Also by Jacci Turner

THE BIRTHRIGHT SERIES
The Cage
The Bar
The Lamb

THE FINDING HOME SERIES
Bending Willow
Stretching Willow
Finding Willow
Willow's Ride
Willow's Roundup

YOUNG ADULT
Cracker
Snapped

OTHER
Shipwrecked

TREE
SINGER

Jaclyn,
Enjoy !
Jaci Turner
Love your name ♡

JACCI TURNER

Lucky Bat Books

A Lucky Bat Book

Tree Singer
Copyright 2021 Jacci Turner
Cover Design: E.R.Canedo

ISBN: 978-1-943588-91-6

LuckyBatBooks.com
10 9 8 7 6 5 4 3 2 1

To David, my love.
In the trees with you—always.

CHAPTER ONE

Mayten lay with her legs stretched along the sturdy limb of her favorite oak tree, the smooth bark cool against her bare legs, the rougher patches prickling her skin. She pressed her back against the thick trunk and turned her face upward as if trying to catch the sun's warmth, the earthy woodiness of the oak tree tickling at her nose. The gnarled limbs overhead reminded her of a child with arms akimbo, jutting out from the trunk in every direction.

There was beauty in the chaos above her, sunlight weaving its way through the branches like a blessing, birds twittering invisible among the leaves.

She'd always felt at peace sitting in her auntie tree, usually with a good book, but sitting and thinking was just as peaceful.

Until today.

She'd come to the tree this morning for selfish reasons, nervous about the upcoming ceremony. She was fifteen now and would be leveling up tomorrow. Today was the last chance she'd have to simply 'chat' with her beloved auntie tree. She'd poured out her hurt and pain and worry just as she had for as long as she could remember.

Perhaps because she was leveling up or just growing up, for the first time Mayten actually received an answer. Not in words.

In *feelings.*

A rush of confusing emotions that threatened to curl her into a tiny ball.

She didn't know what the auntie tree was trying to tell her, but there was a surety in Mayten's bones that something was deeply wrong with her beloved trees. Not just her auntie tree.

With all the trees.

Mayten placed trembling hands on the branch beneath her, trying to ignore the way her belly churned, trying to *feel* what the tree was saying.

Trying to understand.

Listening to the trees wasn't easy. Listening took focused concentration. Which was why the youngest singers spent all their time talking to the trees.

The time for talking is over, she reminded herself. Tomorrow she would begin her Level Four training. She'd learn to not only send but to *receive* feelings, to truly communicate with the trees.

Judging by the intensity of emotions sent from the tree, she needed to understand now. If she could understand what Auntie was trying to tell her, Mayten could pass the message along to her mother and her clan could fix whatever was wrong.

Mother is busy preparing for the Leveling Ceremony, a tiny voice whispered at the back of her mind.

Yes, Castanea was the clan's chief tree singer and she *was* busy preparing for the Leveling Ceremony. But surely she would make time to listen to her daughter.

Wouldn't she? It seemed as though her mother had been avoiding her lately.

Time enough to worry about her mother later, Mayten decided. Right now she needed to try again. See if she could figure out what was wrong with the trees.

She firmly closed her mind to the outside world in much the same way she closed her bedroom door. Closed out the sun's warmth on her face. Closed out the chatter of squirrels amid a flutter of birds' wings.

Then she pulled a mental curtain shutting out the insects buzzing about her head and sounds of laborers out in the fields calling to one another as they worked.

And focused on her auntie tree.

Remembering the storm of emotions, she cautiously opened both mind, then soul to whatever message the tree was trying to send.

It seemed to take an eternity, but she knew it was only seconds before her gut tightened with anxiety. Once again emotions exploded in her skull like sparks from a fire, a jumble of feelings she couldn't identify cascading along her skin, flooding through her body . . .

"Auntie?" she whispered. She didn't understand. Couldn't connect what she was feeling with any sort of message —

Mayten cried out as the emotional storm intensified, striking her with stinging blows from all sides like hail from a midsummer storm. Leaving her shaking and uncertain.

"Mayten? Mayten!"

Her little brother's voice knifed through her concentration and focus like a bolt of lightning, shredding the emotions and scattering them to the wind. Mayten startled, almost toppling from the branch. She struggled to cling to the memory of all those emotions, to somehow fix them in her mind so she could discuss them with her mother later . . .

The emotional storm faded, drifting away like dying sparks on a breeze. All she could remember of the message—if it had been a message—was what it wasn't. It wasn't pain she'd felt. And it wasn't exactly fear—

She rose to her feet, knees shaking, and steadied herself with a hand against the trunk. "Sorry, Auntie. I've got to go. I'll come back when the ceremony's over."

Mayten's heart twisted. After tomorrow, there would be no more time for childish chats. Tomorrow she would begin her life's work.

Levels One through Three were easy as far as she was concerned. Talking to trees came naturally to her. Her mother, apparently, expected Mayten's listening skills to come just as easily. She'd lost count of the number of times her mother had reminded her to 'stop *talking* to the trees and start *listening!*'

Listening was proving to be the most difficult thing Mayten had ever tried—

"Are you coming down?" Wollemi jogged up to the tree and looked at her expectantly. "It's eventide and Mother says to come in."

Mayten studied her little brother. He was a sight, his brown homespun pants and shirt hanging off his small frame like the hand-me-downs they were. She could tell by his flushed skin—skin the color of weak tea—he'd been running. His little nose wrinkled, squishing his dark freckles into tiny specks as he gazed up at her.

Her mother had birthed two babies before Wollemi was born. Both had died during the fever winter. Mother had two more babies following Wollemi. Helping care for the babies wore Mayten out, but Wollemi made her efforts worthwhile.

"I'm coming." She grinned down at her brother, warmth spreading from her heart, relaxing her muscles, sending her worry scampering off into the distance. She scrambled down the trunk of the tree without even looking for a foothold.

Eventide? How had that happened? The sun was slipping away and she hadn't even noticed.

When she jumped to the ground, Wollemi grabbed her hand with his pudgy little one and they marched up the hill.

"Are you worried about the ceremony?" Her brother raised his eyebrows, brown eyes dark and serious.

"No, not for me," she finally said. "But I am worried about Tray."

Mayten swallowed the lump suddenly clogging her throat. If all went as planned, her best friends would level up tomorrow as well.

And everything would change.

She, Tray, and Cather had been best friends since birth. On the morrow, Cather would be called to be a healer like her parents but Tray wanted adventure. Tray's dreams of being a traveler would be fulfilled, Mayten was certain of that. It was what he wanted, and she wanted it for him as did Cather.

"Because he'll be called a traveler or a quester and leave you and Cather at home without him?" Wollemi asked.

Mayten marveled at Wollemi's insight. How could her brother be so young and yet so keenly in touch with her worries?

Wollemi's pink tongue pushed through the hole where his front tooth had been only two days earlier and his eyes sparkled with excitement. "Maybe . . . maybe you'll be a story singer like Taiwania or a *quest taker!*"

Mayten ruffled her little brother's wild brown curls. He knew the story singers were valued in the community, almost as much as the questers, those brave men and women who explored beyond the clan.

"I'm a tree singer," she said in a firm voice. She *was* a tree singer, like her mother, grandmother, and great-grandmother. A surge of pride washed over her. She hailed from a family of singers. Singers helped the plants grow, thrive, and take shape.

Her da sang flowers and shrubs, and her older brother, Oleaster, sang the harvest.

"I've always wanted to be a tree singer, nothing else. As tree singer, I'll get to stay here forever and that means I'll never be taken from you."

She stopped walking and pulled Wollemi in for a tight hug. She felt close to all of her siblings, except for Taiwania, but she felt extra protective of Wollemi.

Voices from somewhere ahead caught her attention. Mayten glanced at the house crouching among a sea of yellow daffodils overlooking the clan's valley. Perched on a small hill, the house that had started as a one-room cottage had been added to as their family had grown, and grown, and grown. Great wings—designed by the clan's wood crafters and lovingly built—fanned to either side of the original structure, stretching into the garden of stunning spring flowers.

Da had sung those flowers, making sure their home was constantly surrounded by blossoms that budded and bloomed at different times of the year. She drew in the sweet scent of honeysuckle, anticipating the time when tulips of every imaginable color, and some colors only her da could imagine, would carpet their hill.

A breeze lifted her hair, bringing with it the spicy tang of eucalyptus. She loved the forest of oak and eucalyptus bordering the house and garden on the left. Oleaster's bountiful groves of fruit and nut trees stood in a line to the right of their home.

Beyond the house and garden, stretching to the base of the pine forest, grew the flowers and shrubs her da raised for trade along with the pine seedlings her mother planted to replace the forest cuttings.

Mayten loved her home. She couldn't imagine being anywhere else. She had no desire to be a quester. No desire to leave. Not ever.

Wollemi hugged her hard, then stepped away, taking her hand in his again. "Then tonight when I sing to my stars, I'll sing for you to be a tree singer!"

"Thank you." Mayten nodded at the house. "Looks like Mother tired of waiting."

An enormous dog bounded down the hill toward them. His tan-and-white chest heaved as he ran, pink tongue flapping, and curly tail bouncing, barreling toward them like a wild boar on attack. The dog drew near, then suddenly circled behind them and barked at their heels.

"All right, Anatolian, we're coming, we're coming." Mayten laughed as she and Wollemi raced the rest of the way up the hill.

CHAPTER TWO

The smell of baking bread made Mayten's stomach growl as they stepped into the house. Da was baking his famous rolls for the morrow's breakfast. She spied her father at the long wooden table, reading near the woodstove with her youngest brother cradled on his lap.

This was one of her favorite sights—Da in the kitchen filled with memories of family around the table, laughing and talking together. The setting sun cast an orange glow through lace curtains hanging in the open window, dappling the far wall with patterns of light.

"Da, have you seen Mother?"

"No," he glanced up and his face lit with a warm smile. "I'm sure she's somewhere. Wollemi, I'm sorry to make you the messenger boy, but would you mind getting Oleaster? He's back in his garden."

"I'll get him," Wollemi said with a smile before dashing back out the door.

"Mayten, will you change this one, please? It's almost time for thanks-giving." Da held her littlest brother up for her to take.

Mayten grabbed the chubby little boy who was heavy with sleep and definitely needed changing. She carried him down the hall to the room they used as a nursery.

After the fever winter, the clan leaders had made a new ruling, something that rarely happened. They dictated that families should not name their babies until they were two years old. As a result, Mayten had two unnamed siblings. Privately, she thought of the boy in her arms as Aster and the youngest baby girl as Maple, two of her favorite trees.

She kissed the top of the babe's head and quickly changed his soaked diaper. When little Aster was clean and dry, she dressed him in a tiny tunic and trousers and set off in search of her mother.

Her frustration grew the longer she searched. No sign of Mother in the living area or her parents' bedroom or any of the other rooms that branched off the long hall.

Finally, Mayten went into the room she shared with her sister. Taiwania was sitting on her bed, studying a parchment.

"*I'm* in here," Taiwania groaned, her eyes rolling with disgust. The scent of lavender oil stung Mayten's eyes. Had Taiwania bathed in the stuff?

She studied her sister's waist-length hair. Taiwania's hair flowed in waves while Mayten's hair kinked and curled in uncontrollable brown spirals. Where Mayten's body was sharp and angular, Taiwania had a soft, curvy body and large green eyes fringed with black lashes. Her skin was a beautiful red brown that reminded Mayten of cherry wood.

Mayten had once overheard a neighbor say to her mother, "Mayten is beautiful but doesn't know it. Taiwania is beautiful and she'll tell you about it!"

Mayten knew *she* wasn't beautiful, the neighbor had just said that to be kind, but Taiwania *was* beautiful and wouldn't hesitate to tell you about it.

And she'd become even harder to live with since her Leveling Ceremony last spring.

Usually Leveling Ceremonies proceeded in the same manner each year. The clan elders sequestered themselves for a few days to determine the calling of each apprentice. The callings were in line with the callings of the parents.

But once in a great while, the calling came as a surprise . . .

As had happened with Taiwania. Her sister had been called, not to sing to living things, but to sing the stories of the clan, an essential role in the life of the community.

That day the entire clan had cheered. That day Mayten had seen the pride in her parents' shining eyes, had herself felt a mixture of pride and envy at the way people looked at her sister, especially the boys.

Overnight, Taiwania had become something other than the bossy older sister that Mayten knew, someone treated with honor by the entire clan.

The attention had made Taiwania even bossier and more impossible than she'd been before.

"I need to practice for the ceremony tomorrow, so please leave." Taiwania flicked her hand as if shooing a mosquito away.

"It's my room, too." Mayten flopped on top of her bed's feathered comforter and tickled Aster's cheek, trying to get him to smile. She was frustrated at not finding her mother and the butterflies in her stomach made her feel sick. "Since you'll be singing to the clan tomorrow, you may as well get used to singing in front of people."

She was not afraid to receive her calling, but she hated being the focus of attention and having to stand before the whole clan. Taiwania, however, loved being the center of attention—

"Mother!" Taiwania bellowed, her face darkened with rage. "Will you make Mayten leave the room so I can practice?"

Moments later, their mother stepped into the room, their baby sister strapped to her chest with an intricately tied piece of cloth. "What's the problem here?"

Her mother looked tired. Dark circles shadowed her eyes. Maybe she wasn't avoiding Mayten. Maybe she was sick and trying to hide it.

Taiwania crossed her arms, her mouth puckered like she'd been sucking on an unripe persimmon. "I need to practice my song for tomorrow, and Mayten won't leave."

"But she'll be singing in front of people tomorrow," Mayten protested. "Why not practice in front of someone tonight?"

Her mother blew brown corkscrews of hair off her forehead. "Mayten, give your sister some time to practice tonight. Just until bells. Now come. It's time for thanks-giving."

Mayten balanced Aster on her hip as they followed their mother out the door. "Mother, I need to talk to you —"

Her mother put a hand on the small of Mayten's back, pushing her gently up the hallway.

"Not now," she said, her voice sharp.

Mother never spoke sharply. Not to Mayten. Her throat tightened.

Taiwania put her nose in the air as she pranced by, pushing through the front door first.

Mayten stopped on the threshold, swallowing a desire to slap the smug look off Taiwania's face. She shifted her attention to their mother instead, watching as her mother slipped off her sandals before following Taiwania outside.

Mayten took after her mother, tall and stick thin, with a plain face and skin the washed-out color of walnuts. She'd often wished she had her mother's confidence as well. Instead, she had her da's shy nature and enjoyed being by herself among the trees.

"Mayten," her mother called. "Stop daydreaming and get out here."

Mayten quickly slid off her sandals and hurried out onto the porch, down the wooden steps, and into the front yard where she took her place in the family circle. The cool earth beneath her toes sent a shiver up her spine. She inhaled deeply, tasting eucalyptus spice on her tongue.

Da took little Aster from her arms, settling their youngest brother on his shoulders, then taking Mayten's right hand. She reached out, taking her little brother Wollemi's hand in her left hand. Wollemi grinned up at her, poking his tongue through the empty space between his teeth. Mother stood next to him gently swaying from side to side, calming the babe strapped to her front. Then came Taiwania with Oleaster completing the circle.

Her oldest brother Oleaster was the mirror image of her father and like her da was happiest with his hands in the dirt. Where her father sang their flowers, though, her brother sang their food.

She also had two older sisters—twins—who had married men from the Ocean Clan and had gone to live by the sea. She thought of the twins this time each night. She also thought about the two siblings who had died during that awful winter when fever swept through the clan.

Her da raised his arms, and the family joined him. He looked around at each of them, seeming to drink in each face with such love it made Mayten's heart hurt.

Had his gaze lingered overlong on her face?

It was hard to tell in the lamplight, but she thought his eyes glistened more than usual. He had to clear his throat before speaking the sacred words.

"Our feet are planted in the earth from which we came. Our hands reach to the stars which give us hope. We thank You for all that we have. We trust You for all we have lost." His voice broke, as it did every night. Her da still hurt over the loss of his children and desperately missed his older daughters. Perhaps he was just missing them more tonight. "For everything and everyone between the stars and the earth we give thanks to you, Great Singer."

"We give thanks, Great Singer," Mayten echoed with the rest of her family. She never tired of her da's warm voice.

They lowered their hands, each member going his or her way. Mayten kissed the top of Wollemi's head as Mother came to get him. He squeezed her hand extra hard.

"Tonight," he whispered, "when I sing to my stars, I'll sing for you to be a tree singer!"

She chuckled and kissed him again. What did Wollemi see in the stars? They were beautiful, of course, but he seemed to have the same kind of relationship with stars she had with trees. He'd probably be a star singer, she realized. One of the rare people called to study and understand the stars and the signs and portents they held. A star singer was more unique than a story singer.

She whispered her thanks as her mother pulled him away. "Mother, can we talk . . . ?"

"Not now," her mother snapped as she ushered the smallest ones off to bed.

Stung by her mother's words, Mayten stood rooted in place, the hurt from her mother's rejection staking her to the ground like one of Oleaster's unruly vines.

Taiwania had no trouble moving and neither did Oleaster. Taiwania hurried back into the house as Oleaster grabbed a lantern and headed toward the village. He was seeing a girl, someone he hoped to join with at the next three-clan gathering.

Moths circled the lanterns dangling from the eaves and crickets sang somewhere in the dark but Mayten paid them no heed. She'd done something wrong, though she had no idea what. Something so horrible her mother—

A warm hand fell on Mayten's shoulder and she glanced up to find Da smiling down at her.

"Are you nervous about tomorrow?"

She studied Da's kind face, the deep smile lines around his eyes and mouth made deeper by the shadows.

"I guess I'm a little nervous about having to stand up in front of the whole clan," she finally said. "But Tray and Cather will be with me. I'm sure everything will be fine."

"You're not worried about your calling?"

"No, why should I be? I was born to be a tree singer." At least she could be sure of that. Some people even said that she was the strongest singer in the clan, maybe even stronger than her mother . . . if she ever learned to stop daydreaming.

"All callings are equally important to the life of the clan," said her da, quoting the start of each Leveling Ceremony.

Mayten smiled even though she doubted his words. Everyone knew that questers, travelers, and clan story singers, like Taiwania, were valued above the rest.

Mayten decided she needed a walk. She had to see her best friend. "Da, can I go see Cather? Just for a little while?"

"Tomorrow you'll be making your own choices, so I guess I best get used to letting you go," he said in a tight voice. "I don't know when you grew up. It happened so fast." He kissed her forehead. "Take a lantern with you . . . and take Anatolian . . . and be back before bells."

She laughed and hugged him tight. Before he could change his mind, she snatched a nearby lantern from its hook and hurried toward the village, whistling for Anatolian as she ran.

CHAPTER THREE

The enormous dog bounded toward her, his tan-and-white chest heaving as he ran. Mayten laughed as the dog arched around behind her and barked at her heels.

"Hey, I invited you, silly," she scolded. "No need to push."

The dirt path leading to the clan center flew beneath her feet. Mayten loved to run in the dark. The lantern swung as she ran, illuminating the well-worn path with swaying light. She didn't really need a light. She'd been tromping this path barefoot since she could walk and knew every tree root and slippery place along the way.

The dog seemed delighted in the late outing, sniffing trees and plants along the way. Every other tree or so he stopped to make his mark, then raced to catch up.

The smells changed as Mayten drew closer to the village. Damp forest smells were replaced by the tang of cut lumber and the odor of people living close together. She didn't like the smell, preferring the scent of growing things to those of the village.

Though she knew it was coming, the feel of cool stone beneath her feet shocked Mayten. She slowed to be sure of her footing, listening to the quiet sounds of clansfolk settling in for the night. She preferred the quiet of the village at night when the regular noises of sawing and building—typical for a clan of boatwrights and builders—had ceased.

Anatolian trotted up and stood quietly by her heels as she studied the village, looking for anything new or out of place. Carved out of the forest generations ago, the village radiated outward from the central square in five rings. The square was where the community held its special meals and celebratory dances.

Every third year, when her clan hosted the three-clan gathering, temporary shelters were placed around the outside of the center square, squeezed between buildings, filling the available space throughout the five rings of homes.

The Leveling Ceremony would be held here in the morning. There was plenty of room for the temporary stage dominating the square, its shape large and hulking in the dark.

She much preferred being one of the "hill families" living on the homesteads outside the village. Homesteads were bigger than homes in the clan center and had loads of space in between. The hill families grew things the clan needed, like trees for building, fruits and vegetables for food. Her brother's fruits and nuts were always in demand as were the flowers and shrubs her da grew for trade and the pine seedlings her mother planted to replace the forest cuttings.

The paving stones beneath her feet had been brought in by ships or quarried up on the mountain. The village homes had a uniform look—each with a pointed roof, window boxes, and scrolled window shutters carved with intricate designs. Most were painted white, but some wore pastel colors, and each family had a small garden at the rear of the home.

Cather's family lived close to the village center. The location of their home had more to do with the fact Cather's parents were healers than anything else. They had to be accessible to the villagers as well as the mill where most of the injuries happened. The mill stood right on the shore of the river.

Clansfolk who lived close to the center generally had smaller families, and most of them worked in the mill or in the shipyard. From tree to mill to ship, her clan constructed vessels of all sizes for the other clans as well as for their own use. Larger ships were constructed in sections and floated down the river to the Ocean Clan where they were assembled and launched.

Mayten kept an eye on the street as she worked her way to Cather's home. She enjoyed the way lamplight illuminated each home, but felt like an intruder peeking in the open shutters. She quickened her pace.

Cather's place was just like the other homes except for two distinguishing characteristics—the wooden *Healer* sign above the door and the small room added onto the rear where a garden would typically be. The extra room held several cots where those who needed longer-term care could stay.

Mayten admired the window boxes filled with beautiful flowers from Mayten's family garden, at no charge of course. Her friend's family was always supplied with the choicest of fruits and vegetables, too. That's how the clan worked. People traded for what they needed and little coin ever changed hands. It worked differently between clans and with those who came through on trading ships to exchange goods with the merchants. But within the clan, money wasn't really necessary.

Mayten tapped gently on Cather's door.

"I was hoping you'd come by!" Cather swung the door wide, pulling Mayten into the warm, cozy nest of her home. Mayten gestured at her dog as the door closed and knew that Anatolian would wait outside until she was ready to leave.

She couldn't help comparing her homestead with Cather's home. The homestead was spacious, open, and uncluttered, despite the large number of people who lived there.

Here the rooms always felt crowded with overstuffed furniture and knickknacks on every shelf. Cather's mother could never pass by the trade barges that came up the river without coming back with some new trinket. And she never had the heart to throw anything away.

Cather had often remarked how spare the homestead was, but Mayten loved the clean lines and carved furniture with colorful cushions. She enjoyed the openness of it, sometimes feeling unable to breathe in the closeness of Cather's home.

"Hello, Mayten," Cather's mother said with a smile. She dropped a newly rolled bandage into the large woven basket sitting on the floor beside her. "Excited about tomorrow?"

Cather's father lifted his pipe in greeting and went back to his book. He sat in one of Mayten's favorite chairs—a rocker carved from one of her trees. A fire snapped and popped in the fireplace, adding to the cozy feeling.

"Yes, ma'am . . ." Mayten started, intending to say a proper hello, but Cather tugged on her arm and nodded toward her room.

"Go on, girls. You have little time." Cather's mother winked.

Cather's room was decorated in pinks and peppered with flower prints. The bed took up most of the room, leaving only a small dresser for clothes, a rack for hanging dresses, and some shelves that were full of stuffed animals and trinkets. Cather had lost two siblings, one sister in the fever winter and one older brother in a mill accident, leaving her an only child. Sadness seemed to permeate the very walls of the house. Mayten imagined that to be healers and not be able to save your own children must have made their deaths doubly painful.

"I was afraid you wouldn't come." Cather dragged Mayten onto her bed where the girls sat facing each other. Her straight brown hair cascaded around her pretty heart-shaped face and her skin glowed the color of pine in the lantern light. Her light skin—one of the lightest on the island—told of her family's more recent immigration. "It's nearly bells."

"I know. I think Da only let me come because Taiwania is practicing her song for tomorrow in our room." Mayten grimaced. "I can't stay long. I just wanted to see you before—"

"I know." Cather gripped Mayten's hand. "Tomorrow, everything will . . ."

Her eyes glittered with unshed tears, and she swallowed hard.

Mayten gave her a quick hug. "He'll be okay, Cather. Tray will be home more than he's gone, probably. And you'll still have me."

Her friend swallowed and gave her a weak smile. "I know. It's just—well, I don't want you to—I mean, once we become initiates, we'll be much busier. I won't get to see you as much . . . and I hate that." Cather turned her face away.

Was she nervous about something other than Tray's leaving? If so, why?

Mayten gave a mental shake. She and Cather always told each other everything; she must be imagining it. But Cather had always been sensitive to changes, and the idea that Tray might leave them to go on a quest, was a big change.

Whatever the problem was, they could deal with it later. There were more pressing matters at hand.

"I'm going to need your help," Mayten said. "There's something wrong with the trees, and I can't figure out what it is."

Cather looked up, brown eyes huge. "Did your mother tell you that?"

"No, I sensed it, but I don't know what it is."

A tap on the door made them both jump.

"Cather," her mother called. "It's almost bells and tomorrow's a big day."

Disappointment flooded Mayten. She desperately wanted to talk with someone about the trees, and now there was no time.

"All right, Mama." Cather stood, pulling Mayten to her feet. "Let's pledge that no matter what happens tomorrow, we'll always be friends."

"Of course, why wouldn't we be? But what do I do about the tre—"

Cather threw her arms around Mayten and squeezed hard. "Whatever it is, I'm sure your mother will help you figure it out. You'd better run."

Mayten found herself pulled out of the room almost as abruptly as she'd been pulled in. Cather hurried to the front door and ushered her outside. Mayten waved a quick goodbye to Cather's parents.

"Well, that was strange." Anatolian nudged her hand with a damp nose and trotted along beside her.

What was wrong with Cather? She was usually the steady one in their friendship, the sweet, happy one. Tray loved jokes and games while Mayten was the quietest of their little trio. He also seemed totally unaware of Cather's feelings for him—

The bell in the clan's tower clanged.

"Race you home!" Mayten said, ruffling Anatolian's ears. They both took off at a run, Anatolian pulling ahead with ease.

Mayten risked a glance back at Cather's home. The dark had almost swallowed the building, leaving only the soft glow of lantern light as evidence someone lived there.

Mayten's stomach knotted. She had a strong feeling, the kind of feeling she'd gotten from the trees, something more was going on here. Something other than the possibility of Tray's leaving.

But what could it possibly be?

CHAPTER FOUR

Mayten's family straggled into the community square the next morning as the sun was just peeking over the tops of the trees. Mother and Taiwania had left the homestead even earlier but getting the little ones up and dressed had slowed the family, making Mayten nervous they would be late. She breathed a sigh of relief as other families came in after them.

Savory smells drifted from an assortment of covered dishes displayed on tables arranged in two long lines at the back of the square. Mayten's stomach growled, though she couldn't eat even if she'd wanted to. Da's breakfast rolls sat like bricks in her stomach.

There would be plenty of time to eat after the ceremony when the rest of the clan joined the initiates in a community meal.

The atmosphere reminded her of the solstice gatherings. The air fairly crackled with electricity and there were smiles on everyone's faces.

Long shadows flowed from the large, rectangular stage perched about five feet off the ground with stairs going up each side, the illuminated details stark in the morning light. Mayten stood near the stage with the families of the others who would be leveling up. She shifted nervously from foot to foot until

Oleaster bumped her shoulder with his and gave her a smile that calmed the flutters in her stomach. Wollemi stood in front of her. She hadn't realized she was playing with his hair until he reached up, his small hand wrapping around her fingers.

She didn't know why she was nervous, not really. There was no doubt in her mind she would be the next tree singer . . .

A whisper of emotion touched her mind, the same fear she'd felt from the trees yester eve, and an icy hand clutched at her heart. She wasn't nervous about the ceremony at all, she realized. She was worried about the trees.

When the ceremony was over, she'd speak to her mother no matter how busy her mother claimed to be.

Mayten squeezed Wollemi's hand and chanced a look around the square.

The clan had gathered about the stage, roughly two hundred people standing in family groups. Nine of the clan's own would level up and receive their callings today, becoming adult members of the clan's community.

She could see Cather standing with her mother and father. Her friend looked beautiful in her green dress, the top of her long dark hair tied back with a matching green bow. The clan colors—greens and browns—looked particularly good next to Cather's hair.

The same colors did nothing for Mayten. She glared down at her dull brown pants and tunic. Clan clothing consisted of woven, loose-fitting garments of greens and browns with the adults wearing ceremonial white aprons that signified their callings. Some women wore dresses, but it was perfectly acceptable for a woman to wear loose-fitting pants like the men.

It had never occurred to her to wear a dress—dresses were impractical for tree-climbing singers. Still, it might have been more appropriate.

Cather saw Mayten looking at her and gave her a dimpled smile, nervously twisting the ribbon in her hair. Cather would be called to be a healer like her parents, there was no reason for her to be nervous —

Mayten frowned. Cather's eyes were red, as if she'd been crying. Her parents' eyes looked red too.

Had their family received bad news?

Tray and his parents, four brothers, and three uncles stood in a group just beyond Cather. He was almost as tall as his da, having passed both Mayten and Cather in height this last year, leaving Cather the shortest of the three. He might even be growing into his ears which had always stuck out a bit too far.

Unruly black hair stabbed the air around his head and his almond-shaped eyes sparkled with laughter. His skin looked like creamed coffee. His family were all travelers of various sorts: some traveled on trade ships, some were favored questers who carried the lore of other places and exciting adventures with them when they returned from their quests.

Next to Tray stood his uncle Adven, a famous quester. Mayten shivered as Adven glanced at her with a frown and she looked quickly away.

Adven scared her. He was Tray's da's younger brother, but was nothing like Tray's father. The man seemed to lurk around the edges of the clan, like a cougar you could never quite see but knew was there. With long, shaggy hair, an unshaven face, and a hat that covered one eye, Mayten had never seen him smile.

Adven always made the hair on the back of her neck stand up, yet Tray idolized his uncle and dreamed of being called to be a quester so he could travel with him.

Oleaster bumped her shoulder again and jutted his chin toward the stage. Taiwania stood in the center looking lovelier than ever in a green dress and white apron.

The ceremony was about to begin.

Of course, *Taiwania* had thought to wear a dress. Mayten snuck a glance at Tray, who rolled his eyes and made her smile. He always could cheer her up. She turned her attention back to her sister.

Every year the youngest story singer received the privilege of singing the First Song. The First Song told of the clan's beginning and was exhaustingly long. People spread their blankets and sat cross-legged on the ground, settling in to listen.

Taiwania had a beautiful voice, though Mayten hated to admit it. She didn't envy her sister the position of story singer, though.

Thank the stars I won't be called to be a story singer. She'd much rather be with the trees and would die of embarrassment before she'd stand on a platform and *sing* in front of the entire clan.

There were several older boys who seemed mesmerized by Taiwania. Mayten couldn't blame them. Taiwania's hair was held off her face by a bow the exact color of her dress and her green eyes were unusual for this island. Her apron, impossibly white with its green embroidered scroll on the bib, marked her as a clan story singer.

Whoever ended up as her sister's mate had a big surprise in store, though. Taiwania wasn't all sweetness and light, that was for sure, but she sang very well.

"Come listen to the story of Trigginsfeld and how we came to be." Taiwania's clear, sweet voice carried over the crowd.

Her sister sang of the Ocean Clan, explorers from Elan who found they liked the island life so much they never left. And the Sun Clan, originally Ropian slaves who found freedom when the ships bearing them crashed on the rocks. And prisoners from Sapia who'd been left on the island to die and had founded the Forest Clan instead.

As the clans were established and then intermarried, the skin tones and distinguishing features of the clans blurred into varied shades of brown, with the clansfolk migrating throughout the island to live where their gifts and talents were most needed.

Taiwania embodied a perfect combination of their island home. Her hair looked like that of the original island dwellers—long, raven-black, and wavy. Her skin was the mahogany silk of the freed slaves. Her eyes had the almond shape of the sea traders from Caspia who took a liking to the island, but were green like the Sapian prisoners, and she had the body of an Elanian dancer.

It seemed right she had been called to sing their story, to tell the tale of Trigginsfeld . . .

> *"The trade winds and the currents keep our island fair and warm,*
> *But buried bars of sand and rock, cause ships to come to harm.*
> *Only with the island's help can sailors find their way,*
> *It welcomes those who mean no harm, the rest it drives away."*

This sounded more magical than it was as Mayten well knew. Cliffs and boulders lined the island's far side, making it uninhabitable and too treacherous to be approached by ship.

> *"Three clans there are in Trigginsfeld, three clans to serve the king.*
> *The first great clan are ocean folks, who trade through seafaring.*
> *The second noble sister clan grows fabric for the weave.*

With skilled hands and an artist's eye, designs upon the sleeve.
The third great clan in Trigginsfeld boasts trees beyond compare.
Shipwrights and fine carpenters have skills abundant there."

The three ports of the Sun Clan, the Ocean Clan, and the Castle Keep—where the king's family lived and where his garrison of soldiers were housed—were all impossible to navigate without the help of the island's trained sailors. There were stories of pirates who had gotten through the hazards in the past, however, and had to be fought off.

Taiwania got to the part of the song Mayten liked the best and her heart beat a little faster.

"All three fine clans are kindred of the sea, forest, and sun.
Together we all serve our king, together we are one."

To Mayten's surprise, Taiwania looked directly at her as she sang the final verse.

"Today we call forth nine more friends to join us as we serve.
To bring their gifts as offerings and strengthen us with nerve."

A shiver ran down Mayten's spine.

"All the gifts are needed; here we honor every one."

Taiwania gestured dramatically down from the platform toward those gathered on the ground.

"Come forth you nine and join us now, your calling time has come."

The crowd cheered and jumped to their feet, clapping. The families of the nine initiates dragged the initiates to their feet and pushed them toward the stage. Mayten kissed her tiny siblings, babies too young to understand the intense emotion all around them, and looked frantically at her family.

Oleaster nodded her on, his dark hair flapping as he clapped. Da smiled and waved her forward with his hands. Wollemi gave her a gap-toothed smile as she took a breath and joined Tray and Cather climbing the stairs to the platform. Her palms were damp and she couldn't seem to catch her breath.

Taiwania smiled at each initiate as they climbed the stairs, but when Mayten reached the platform her sister pulled her into a close hug.

Mayten's throat squeezed painfully and she blinked, surprised by her own tears and even more surprised to see her tears reflected in her sister's eyes. She stared as her sister left the stage.

What caused Taiwania's tears? Nerves from having to sing in front of everyone? Relief at being done?

CHAPTER FIVE

Clan leader Solis—tall and regal with skin the color of coffee and short white hair—climbed the stairs on the far side of the stage, driving thought of Taiwania's strange tears from Mayten's mind. The clan leader's white ceremonial gown flowed to the ground and her sleeves hung bell-like around her wrists. The symbols of all the clan callings had been embroidered in vibrant greens and warm browns around the outside of her apron bib while the scroll in the center of the bib proclaimed the wearer to be a singer of all songs.

Solis crossed the stage, stopping beside a table on which nine white aprons lay face down. Mayten's heart skipped a beat. *Her* apron was there amongst the others, all made by the skilled hands of the Sun Clan. Once the initiates donned the aprons of their callings, they would be adults.

She would be an adult.

No more skipping about the woods with Anatolian.

No more sneaking off with Tray and Cather to swim in the pond.

No more carefree mornings complaining to her trees.

Solis held up her hands, white sleeves billowing in the light morning breeze.

"Thank you to our new story singer, Taiwania," she said as the crowd grew quiet. "I don't think I've ever heard the First Song sung so beautifully."

Mayten glanced down at her sister standing with the family, surprised to see her mother had joined them. Taiwania beamed at the clan leader's praise, even though Solis said this to the story singer every year.

The crowd applauded and Mayten joined in, smiling at her sister. She thought about Taiwania's unexpected hug. Maybe there would be a thawing between them now that Mayten was an adult. She thought she might like that.

"All callings are equally important to the life of the clan," Solis continued. "Unless we work together, we will not have all we need to live safe, strong, and free."

Every year, the clan leader declared all callings equal, yet Mayten couldn't help but feel that some callings were more valued than others. Story singers were rare and most of the clan's leaders had been singers of stories.

She dared a look at the crowd and then lifted her gaze to the south beyond the rows of homesteads. It was miles down the path to the far-off Ocean Clan but she imagined her oldest sisters, living with their new husbands, standing with the men's extended families at a ceremony much like this and wearing the blues and greens of the Ocean Clan. How many new initiates did their adopted clan have today? What about the Sun Clan?

She looked east, picturing the Sun Clan initiates in yellow and orange clothes, colors she would love to wear.

She longed for the solstice celebration this summer when the three clans came together. She couldn't wait to see her sisters and their families. The celebration was filled with trading and dancing and—for those who were sixteen like Taiwania— opportunities to look for future mates.

Taiwania pretended not to care about that opportunity, but Mayten knew she secretly looked forward to it. Her sister dismissed the attention from boys in their clan, claiming a better choice lived elsewhere.

Mayten had no interest in finding a mate and was glad to have another year pass before that expectation came her way. Maybe she would never join with a mate. Some clan members chose that option.

For those like Oleaster who had already chosen a mate, the three-clan gathering brought an opportunity to declare their intentions before the clans. The newly declared couple would work together to build their homestead, or, in her brother's case, to add on to her family's home. When the building was complete, a wedding ceremony—the Joining—would be held. People brought gifts to that ceremony, items that helped the new couple set up their home.

Mayten felt glad for her brother as she knew he was eager to be Joined.

Suddenly, Mayten felt the initiates shift beside her. Faces in the crowd showed puzzlement and concern rather than expectation.

"I want to speak to the rumors some have heard concerning a blight coming to the land." Solis clasped her hands in front of her, her expression serious.

Blight?

Confused, Mayten glanced at her mother—who refused to meet her gaze. Castanea stayed focused on Solis.

Her mother *had* been avoiding her, she felt sure of it now. If there were rumors, her mother would have known.

A blight meant something was attacking the land, destroying the growing things. Insects, disease, or drought could cause a blight. The trees would surely feel that.

Why the secrecy? If she was being trained as an initiate, she should have been told about everything that concerned the trees.

"I'm afraid the rumors are true," the clan leader said.

A gasp ran through the crowd and people murmured to one another. Mayten darted a glance at Cather, who didn't look surprised.

Solis raised her arms and the crowd stilled. "There is no cause for alarm."

Something in the woman's voice made Mayten skeptical.

"We need to investigate further," Solis continued. "We cannot make judgments or decisions about something we know little about. We are forming a special questing team to journey to Castle Trigginsfeld and possibly beyond to gather information."

The crowd gasped again. Questers rarely went beyond the king's castle. Castle Trigginsfeld defined the western border of the clans and was almost a week's journey. And the king had troops, an army, and plenty of questers who reported directly to the king.

Why would he need their help?

Mayten felt Tray stiffen next to her. He turned west—toward the forest and the king. Of course he'd want to go, despite the fact that the western forest was full of dangerous animals and who knew what else.

She knew the forest around them as well as she knew her own home, but Mother had never taken her beyond their clan boundaries into the western forest, saving it for her formal training.

A knot tightened in the pit of Mayten's stomach. She glanced at Cather, whose eyes were shiny with tears. Cather knew Tray would be dying to go—and it was killing her friend.

"To that end, I'd like to change the order of our ceremony and save, until last, the members from our initiates who will join this quest." Solis's words seemed to hang in the air.

Members? Initiates? Why would they be sending initiates and who would be going?

Tray, that was a given. But surely not Cather?

To Mayten's surprise Cather looked almost hopeful. Would her gentle friend be willing to go on a quest just to stay near Tray?

Mayten's shoulders drooped. Of course. Cather would do anything to stay near Tray, even though he was clueless about how she felt. Boys could be so slow sometimes! But if Cather got called to the quest, Mayten would be left alone.

She'd braced herself to lose Tray . . . but Cather too?

It took all Mayten's willpower not to rub at the sudden pain in her chest.

Commotion near the back of the crowd caught her attention. It looked like a small wave of blue was pushing through the brown and green. The wave resolved into the forms of people wearing blue. The figures—two women—worked their way to the front and stood with her family.

It took a moment for Mayten to recognize the pair smiling up at her.

Acerola and Zigba, her twin sisters!

Had they walked all the way from the sea to be here for Leveling Day?

For a brief moment, relief replaced the anxiety bubbling inside. She breathed deeply, as if coming up for air after spending too much time underwater. It was unusual for scattered family members to make a long trek for Leveling Day. How sweet of them to come.

That's when she noticed both twins had their toast-colored arms wrapped around their swollen bellies.

CHAPTER SIX

Mayten felt her jaw drop. She'd forgotten about the letter announcing the pregnancies. The twins did everything together, even joining with the Ocean Clan brothers standing next to them.

Her eyes burned with unshed tears. It likely took them at least two days and probably more to walk here in their current condition.

The twins hadn't returned for Taiwania's Leveling Day, having recently joined with their mates and moved to the ocean. Had they arrived in time to hear their sister sing?

Or did they plan to stay and deliver their babies here with Mother's help? Castanea knew a thing or two about birthing babies, that was certain.

Joy bubbled up in Mayten's stomach. No matter. Whatever had brought her sisters home, their presence was a comfort to her.

And if they had their babies, it would be a welcome distraction from the loss of her friends. But the thought of helping care for more babies drained the energy from her limbs. She was tired of babies. She didn't think she'd ever want babies of her own, having helped care for so many siblings.

"Birla Logger," Solis said as a chunky girl stepped up and stood quietly before the clan leader.

What had Mayten missed? Why couldn't she stay focused?

She glanced up and down the line, shocked to discover four initiates were standing on the other side of the stage, fingering their aprons proudly.

Solis slipped an apron over Birla's head. The bib on it was blank. That was not unusual. A blank bib meant that the initiate would be given more time to find her true calling.

Acerola and Zigba had received blank bibs during their Leveling Ceremony. Those aprons now sported a set of scales. The twins had discovered they were better at making and selling things than they were at singing.

Birla took her place next to the four initiates who'd received their aprons.

Leaving four waiting to be called.

Names were usually called in order of the surname but Cather had just been skipped.

Mayten's heart dropped. Cather's eyes were glistening again but her face glowed with joy.

It was true then. Her gentle friend had gotten her wish— Cather would be going with Tray.

Mayten frowned and tried to ignore the stinging hurt. Hard to accept that Tray was more important to Cather than her best friend. Cather glanced at her, then spun away, her face blushing red.

Only three left to receive aprons: Digby Merchant, Mayten Singer, and Tray Traveler.

Solis hadn't said how many members would be going—

Mayten started as Digby's name was called and he moved forward to receive his apron. He stared proudly down at the symbol of his trade, a set of scales, embroidered on the bib of the apron.

Her own apron would have an oak tree, Cather's a pair of healing hands, while Tray's apron would have a boot for traveling.

That left Cather, Mayten, and Tray on stage. Cather moved closer to Mayten's side and took her hand. The warm, familiar touch gave her small comfort. Mayten grabbed Tray's large hand, damp with sweat. This might be the last time they stood together as friends.

She swallowed her sadness and waited for her name to be called.

Solis turned to them, hands outstretched, palms up. "These three initiates have been chosen to go on our quest."

Mayten glanced over her shoulder, sure that she had missed someone, but the stage behind her was empty.

There must be some kind of mistake. Tree singers don't go on quests.

She glanced at her mother, who met her eyes. Mother's jaw was set in a manner Mayten had seen before—when her mother was giving birth and refused to cry out in pain. Her da had tears streaming down his face, as did the twins and Taiwania.

Taiwania, crying for her?

Oleaster's jaw looked like granite, but his eyes shone as he looked up at her. Only little Wollemi gazed at her with unabashed joy.

A low murmur rose as the crowd shifted restlessly. Solis raised her hands for silence.

"I know you are wondering," she began, "why a tree singer has been called to go on a quest and why choose three so young?"

"Yes, why?" someone shouted.

Mayten's hand started to raise on its own. She had to interrupt Solis, had to tell her she would most definitely *not* be going on this quest—

"It is through our oldest and most gifted tree singer, Castanea," Solis said, gesturing at Mayten's mother, "that we became aware of the blight attacking our land. The trees have been our most reliable messengers and will, I dare say, continue to be so. Therefore, a tree singer is needed on this quest. Although Castanea was eager to join the quest, the council has decided against it. We need her leadership here at this time. She has nominated her daughter Mayten to take her place."

Mayten stared down at her mother in shock. She didn't know what made her angrier, that her mother had volunteered to leave them and go off on some quest, leaving her family—with Mayten caring for the babies, no doubt—or that her mother had suggested Mayten go in her place.

Their gazes locked. Her mother was trying to communicate something. "Don't let me down? Don't embarrass me? Don't make them regret my decision?"

Mayten clenched her jaw until it ached. She couldn't go. She didn't know how to help. She only knew how to sing three of the seven levels.

But she would not let her mother see her knees shaking.

She breathed in slowly through her nostrils and shifted her gaze back to Solis.

"All our experienced questing teams are out gathering information about the blight. These three initiates come from families with excellent gifts in their callings. All three have completed their first three years of training with excellent marks. And, just as importantly, have been friends since birth. They know each other. They trust each other, which is a quality that can take questing teams years to develop."

It felt strange to realize she had been discussed by the council. But not as strange as Solis's next words.

"The king himself has requested our help—immediately."

Again, the crowd shifted and muttered. Mayten glanced at her friends who looked as worried as she felt.

Had the king ever requested the help of her clan before? Of any clans? Yes, he relied on their tribute and in exchange provided protection, laws, and order, but to ask for help . . . to *personally* request help?

It chilled her bones to think their kingdom—which had always been strong and safe—had somehow become vulnerable.

A shudder ran down her back as she suddenly understood why the twins had trekked all that way.

They had come to say goodbye.

Everything tumbled into place—her father's sadness and her mother's avoidance. They'd known.

And hadn't told her.

The clan leader raised her hands once again and silence fell. "To offset the team's inexperience, the quest will be led by Adven himself."

Mayten straightened in disbelief as Tray's uncle, scruffier than ever, bowed to the clan leader.

The crowd cheered as Mayten groaned under her breath.

Solis gracefully inclined her head, acknowledging Adven's bow. "He has, at my request, returned prematurely from a different quest to the south and assures me he is eager to serve this call. We thank you, Adven," she said, inclining her head once again.

"We thank you, Adven," the crowd echoed, the words growing to a roar.

Mayten's stomach squeezed tight, feeling as though someone had punched her. This couldn't be happening. She began breathing through her nose as the warmth drained from her face. She would not faint. Not here in front of everyone.

Solis turned to the initiates. Mayten felt she might be sick as the leader's deep brown eyes held her gaze for a long moment before shifting to Tray, then to Cather.

"What say you, Initiates?" Solis's voice rang clear and strong. "Will you accept the call to this quest for your clan and for your king?"

Tray jumped forward in his excitement. "I will!"

A ripple of laughter went through the crowd.

Cather stood tall. "I will." Her voice quavered but sounded resolute.

Silence stretched as the leader turned again to Mayten. Solis's eyes were steel gray, she realized. Eyes that asked no question.

Only one answer would be acceptable to the clan leader . . .

And the rest of the clan.

Heat flushed Mayten's face. What would happen if she said no? Her eyes flicked to her family. Her mother's face was set, as if willing her to be strong. Her da and siblings brushed tears away.

But it was little Wollemi's face that caused her to pause. His gaze held pure happiness and pride. In his eyes there was no greater honor for his sister than to be called a quester.

She glanced at Cather, who seemed to be pleading with her to say yes. Taking a steadying breath, Mayten straightened her shoulders. "I will."

Her voice squeaked like a mouse, but it seemed enough for Solis. The clan leader raised her arms high and bowed toward them. "Thank you, Initiates."

"Thank you, Initiates!" roared the clan, erupting into loud cheers and shouts.

CHAPTER SEVEN

Da's gentle fingers pulled the plaits of Mayten's braids tight as he twisted her curls up off her neck. It had been years since he had offered to braid her hair and she leaned into his hands, longing to cuddle up in his lap like she had when she was little.

Instead, she sat on a stool as her da stood over her, deftly braiding her hair in front of a large looking glass he had imported from Sapia.

They were in her parents' bathing room, a room unique to their home. It had been Oleaster's idea to use the irrigation system he'd invented, channeling water from a wooden trough that lay in the creek above the homestead through bamboo pipes down to their home and through the walls into a large wooden barrel opposite the bathing room door. A similar barrel stood outside the kitchen wall.

A fireplace in one corner held a large kettle where they warmed the water, then added it to the spring water in the huge tub Oleaster had talked Da into special ordering from the traders.

"You really should forgive your mother, you know," Da said. "She was just trying to do what is best for the clan and for her family."

Mayten eyed him in the mirror and said nothing. She fingered the boot embroidered next to the tree on her apron.

It had been two days since the calling ceremony, days spent in frantic preparation as the clan leader urged them to hurry. Da had traded flowers for a backpack, her sisters gathered nuts and dried fruit for her supplies, and even Wollemi had given her his lucky rock to take on the journey, the rock with white lines running through it in the shape of a star.

When she was not packing, she visited with her twin sisters, catching up on the news from the Ocean Clan, laughing at their stories. Taiwania laughed with them, everyone trying hard to ignore the impending departure.

Everyone but her mother . . .

"There," Da said, giving her hair a light pat.

Mayten gazed at her reflection. He had parted her hair down the middle from forehead to back and wrangled her twisty hair into two plaits that started in the front and curved around each side of her head, ending in two braids.

Her stomach trembled. She gave Da a shaky smile, feeling more like a deer surrounded by a pack of wolves than a quester.

"I'll be okay," she said, trying to sound convincing.

He nodded and bent to kiss the top of her head, quickly brushing away a tear. It was time. The sky grew lighter outside the window. They were gathering in the clan square at morning bells. The questing team would leave from there.

They'd been briefed yesterday. She, Tray, and Cather along with Adven and the woodsman had stood before the clan elders in the community lodge. The meeting room was small with the elders' six chairs lining one side. Mayten stood next to Cather, trying to keep her knees from shaking.

Solis began. "You all know why we are here. Chief Singer, please brief this team."

Her mother stood and Mayten looked down at her feet. She didn't care if it made her mother look bad. She felt betrayed and wasn't about to pretend otherwise. Why had she been kept in the dark about this?

Why was she the one who had to leave home?

"The trees are in distress," her mother said, her voice quivering. "The cause is . . . unknown. None of our ancient stories tell of a situation such as the one we now face. This is why we need more information and we need it fast."

Mayten's head swam as though the world had tilted slightly.

Her beloved trees were hurting.

She grabbed Cather's hand. They were being sent into unknown danger, with someone in charge that Mayten didn't trust.

Worse, she was expected to do a job she wasn't qualified for . . .

∅

The rest of the day had passed too quickly. She'd barely slept.

And now it was time.

She slid from the stool, checking that her leather boots were tied tightly. Her new socks, knitted by Zigba, made the boots feel snug and would protect her feet from blisters. She wore her sturdiest climbing clothes and carried a change of clothing in her pack.

"Ready?" Da asked.

Mayten nodded, swallowing the lump in her throat.

Da led her out to the porch where the rest of the family waited. The gray dawn seemed to match her dread.

Oleaster stepped up, carrying her pack. He held it out as she slid her arms into the straps, then fastened the waist strap, making sure it fit snugly around her hips. Zigba had knitted soft pads that covered the leather straps, keeping the pack from chafing her shoulders.

A bedroll had been tied to the pack's bottom, a tight roll of wool that seemed thoroughly inadequate. The thought of leaving her soft bed and the grim faces of her family made her throat tighten, threatening to cut off her breathing altogether.

Her older brother tapped her under the chin with his index finger and she looked up. His smile gave her courage. Anatolian sniffed the pack as if it were a stranger. He rubbed his head against her hip. How could she leave her dog? How could she leave any of them?

The family turned together and began the slow walk down the hill toward town, Anatolian trotting alongside. Mayten felt a small hand press into hers and looked down into Wollemi's little face. His freckles stood out against his pale skin like tea leaves floating in a cup. His small forehead wrinkled up at her, concern etching his face.

"Are you scared?" he whispered.

Had it been only three days since her father had asked her the same question about the Leveling Ceremony?

The apprehension she'd felt then seemed like a flea compared to the mountain lion now threatening to tear her apart with terror.

Her world had changed since the ceremony. Three days ago, she'd felt confident of her future, certain of spending the next two years as her mother's initiate.

Now, she felt like a tree severed from its roots. Would parts of her be cut off and shipped to unknown places? Would she ever be whole again?

But she couldn't say that to Wollemi.

"I am . . . a little scared. But if you think of me every time you look at the stars, and I think of you every night, we will still be connected. You will be with me on my journey, don't you see? Nothing can really separate us."

His face relaxed and he skipped a little skip as he walked. "That's a good idea. And I'll know if you're safe because I'll feel it from the stars."

"That's right," she said, and wondered if Wollemi would really be able to feel her through the stars. Did he talk and listen to stars the way she talked and listened to trees?

Her stomach knotted as they approached the community square. It was not as congested as it had been for the Leveling Ceremony, and there were no tables lined with food, no celebratory atmosphere. But there were still a lot of friends and family gathered to sing the questers off.

More people than had come out for any other questing team, of that Mayten felt certain. Was it because three young ones were going or because help had been requested by the king himself?

Cather and Tray stood off to one side, surrounded by their families and friends. Adven looked up as Mayten and her family approached. He eyed her without smiling, then looked away as if to dismiss her.

As far as she knew, a tree singer had never been on a quest. Was he mad he had to take her along? Or did he have something against her, personally?

Dread filled Mayten's heart as Solis climbed the stairs to the stage, and, suddenly, she felt like she carried the weight of the entire clan in her pack.

Solis raised her hands, quieting the crowd. She wore normal brown pants and a sleeveless shirt instead of her ceremonial gown, yet her bare arms seemed to carry as much authority as the gown. "Questers, say goodbye to your families."

Mayten's blood turned to ice. Things were happening too fast. She had been hoping that the king would send a messenger and say the team was no longer needed, that the blight had been healed.

But no messenger arrived.

Large hands grabbed her shoulders and pulled her into a powerful hug. She breathed Da's scent of pipe tobacco and fresh soil and her eyes burned.

He pulled back and looked at her with shining eyes. "You are in my heart, Mayten."

"You are in my heart, Da," she said, her voice tight.

Oleaster hugged her next, but when he said, "You are in my heart, Mayten," his voice broke a bit and her heart squeezed in pain.

She could only nod, tears threatening to spill down her cheeks.

Taiwania came up, looking almost shy. So different from her normal, arrogant approach.

"Next moon, at the gathering, I'll dedicate a song to you," she promised as she hugged Mayten quickly. "You're in my heart."

She moved away and Mayten realized her sister didn't see her coming home by the next moon gathering. A shiver ran down her arms.

The twins stepped up together.

"When you return, you might have new babies to hold," Acerola said.

"We'll stay until you return," Zigba added.

Mayten hugged her sisters gratefully. Her sisters' husbands stepped in a bit awkwardly. Each gave her a quick hug and moved away.

Then came the little ones, Aster and Maple, too young to understand what was happening. Would they even know her when she returned?

If I return.

She shoved the thought away and bent to little Wollemi.

"You are in my heart, Mayten," he said, trying to be brave. But his trembling lips betrayed him.

"You will always be in my heart," she replied. "And I'll meet you at the stars every night." She hugged him hard against her, breathing in his little boy smell of milk and unwashed ears.

Then her mother stood before her. She looked exhausted, her expression hard.

"You are in my heart, Mayten," she said, giving her daughter a stiff hug. She leaned close and spoke words only Mayten could hear. "I know you are mad at me and I don't blame you. But hear this, I would not have recommended you for this journey if I did not have complete confidence in you."

She pulled back, tucking a small book into Mayten's hands. Mayten recognized it at once. It was the brown, leather-bound book her mother used during training, a book traditionally passed down from one tree singer to the next.

At the end of their training.

It should have been two years before Mayten's training was complete. She gripped the book hard. "You're wrong, Mother. I'm not ready. How can I help them when I don't even know how to feel with the trees? I need more time."

"The trees will teach you, Mayten. Listen to the trees. You've always had the talent. I know you can do this."

Mayten looked at her dust-coated boots as her mother continued. "I've decided to send Anatolian with you."

Joy surged through her as she glanced up, searching her mother's eyes. "Truth? You'll let him come with me?"

Anatolian's cold nose tickled her palm.

Her mother nodded. "He will protect you and remind you that you are not alone. Your family's heart goes with you and we will be here when you return."

Mayten studied her mother's lined face. Mother believed they would come back, that *she* would come back. She felt her anger ease just a little. Anatolian was an important part of their family's safety; he had run mountain lions and bears off the homestead more than once.

It was a sacrifice to send the dog . . . and to entrust her with the book. "Thank you, Mother."

Solis's voice rose again. "It is time," she said. And began to sing.

"As you journey, we go with you . . ."

The rest of the clan joined in.

"You don't venture out alone."

Adven beckoned. Mayten lifted her hand in a brief wave to her family, then touched Anatolian's head. The big dog followed her to where Adven stood apart from the crowd, waiting.

Cather stumbled up and grabbed Mayten's hand. Her usually cheerful face was blotchy and red. Mayten glanced at Cather's parents. They wept without shame. She was their last child.

And she was leaving them.

Adven turned without a word and headed away from the village, his friend Hunter striding quietly by his side. Mayten had not been formally introduced to the man. She only knew he was to be their woodsman.

She had seen him around, of course. Their clan rarely entertained strangers. But he was older and Mayten had never spoken to him. She watched him out of the corner of her eye as he walked next to their new leader. His skin was even lighter than Cather's. Red freckles covered what she could see of his skin and his hair was the color of rust.

Tray walked behind the men. She knew from his skipping stride he was practically leaping with happiness.

She and Cather brought up the rear, Anatolian by their side.

Song followed them down the road, fading as the distance grew.

> *"Know that you are not forgotten. We await your safe return."*

Mayten swallowed hard, trying not to let the panic rising in her throat embarrass her in front of the whole clan. Cather squeezed her hand and Anatolian walked so close he brushed against her leg.

> *" 'Till the time we're reunited, carried here upon our song. We trust you to the good Creator . . ."*

The voices took on an ethereal quality as the group approached the trees and stepped into the chill of the forest. She finished the song in her mind as the sound faded.

> *". . . who'll keep you safe from every wrong."*

The path narrowed and they settled into single file with Adven in the lead, followed by Hunter, Tray, Cather, and Mayten, Anatolian at her side. The song echoed in her mind. Would the Creator keep them safe from every wrong?

A shiver ran down her spine. She hoped so, but at this very moment, it was difficult to trust in something she couldn't see. She let her hand rest on Anatolian's head, taking comfort in his warm presence.

CHAPTER EIGHT

That first day was rather boring. All they did was walk, walk, walk. The forest grew darker, trees pressing close about them. She wasn't familiar with these trees, though she'd read about a few of the different types. The gnarly bark and twisted limbs drew her eye as did the delicate ferns and mosses of different varieties that seemed to grow on everything. The air was filled with rich, loamy smells.

Occasionally, she glimpsed white butterflies flitting through the shadows or slugs yellow as spring daffodils and larger than Da's fingers creeping on a log or across the trail.

Mayten quizzed herself on the names of the plants she knew as well as the abundance of forest life. Anatolian was in dog heaven, ranging off trail to chase a squirrel and rejoining Mayten further along, tail thumping happily.

They nibbled on food as they walked, not stopping for a midday meal. They likely would not have stopped at all if Cather hadn't whispered to Tray that she needed to relieve herself. It took some doing, but Tray finally convinced Adven to grant them a brief rest.

Mayten sat on a fallen tree, resting her tired feet. The boots were soft but she wasn't used to wearing them. Birds, squirrels, and insects made a constant hum. The familiar scent of damp earth and rotting vegetation filled her with a deep reassurance, granting her a moment of calm.

She closed her eyes, focusing on the trees.

"Hello Uncle." She reached out to a nearby pine.

Adven grunted and headed off, putting an end to her attempted communication.

"I'm sorry, Uncle. I have to go."

Cather and Mayten jogged to catch up with the others. She glared at the back of Adven's head. Would it hurt to let them rest for a time?

But Adven didn't appear to know what the word meant.

When it became apparent they wouldn't be stopping anytime soon, Mayten decided to mentally review the last three years of her training. The king was depending on her, after all. Depending on all of them.

She'd started training when she was twelve years old. That year had been largely spent among the trees. Her body had grown tall and lanky, making her feel clumsy and awkward on the ground. She loved spending time with her trees, feeling at one among the branches and leaves as she had for as long as she remembered.

That first year she'd followed her mother on her duties, spending equal time in the fields with her da and later with Oleaster. She'd had to learn to sit still for the first time, either near a tree or in one. She had to "let go" of her childish fidgeting and learn the feel, the smell, and even the taste of each tree.

At night Mother would quiz her on the names, medicinal properties, and particularities of each tree as they sat by the fire in the winter or on the porch during warm summer evenings.

She'd grown even taller, passing Taiwania in height during her thirteenth year. Mother encouraged her to go out alone and spend time talking to the trees. Mayten poured out her joys and sorrows to her tree friends, reveling in this new experience. She shared her concerns about her changing body with its bumps and bleeding and the ups and downs of her friendships with Tray and Cather. She railed about the fights she'd gotten into with Taiwania.

The old Auntie tree near their homestead had rivaled Cather as her closest confidante that year, receiving a majority of her time.

Mayten sighed at the memory, then shifted the straps on her shoulders, adjusting the handmade pads, and tried not to think about her aching feet. Instead, she focused on the trees, reaching out and reveling in the feel of new growth.

There was a sweet smell in the air, a smell that had to come from the sugar pines she'd only heard about before. She studied the trees towering high overhead, squinting at the higher branches. Here and there were a few huge cones, long and graceful, cones the trees were famous for. She could barely make out the clusters of new cones hanging at the ends of the branches.

By the end of summer, those babies would be as large as the others, ready to be harvested by frantic squirrels preparing for winter's coming.

The day wore on and Mayten's leg muscles began to ache as much as her feet. Her shoulders burned from the weight of the backpack. She glanced at Cather walking slightly ahead of her. Her friend wasn't used to so much physical exertion but somehow kept moving without complaint.

They began to climb in elevation, her pack seeming heavier with each step. Mayten tried to focus again on the trees. She loved spring when the trees came out of their winter quiet and started to sing about light, and birth, and joy. Familiar comfort washed over her at the feel of moving sap . . .

Mayten gasped as a sense of *wrongness* swept over her. The same sensation that had tickled at the back of her throat when she'd last visited the auntie tree. She peered around, struggling to find what was causing the sensation.

What was wrong with the trees?

The sensation faded, leaving her frustrated. She wasn't prepared for this, she grumbled to herself. How many times had she told Mother she wasn't prepared?

After what felt like an eternity, the terrain changed again. They'd been climbing steadily up a narrow trail cut through pine trees so thick Mayten could barely see between the trunks. Finally, they crested a hill and descended into a canyon, the trees spaced apart as though the forest had decided it needed to breathe. Her spirits lifted as the rich, comforting, homey smell again surrounded her.

Although she could see only a bit of sky, she felt less pressed in. It was cooler here and her muscles relaxed as she descended.

Her heart skipped a beat as she found herself surrounded by beautiful old redwoods with their soft, furry bark. Redwoods were among her favorite trees. She lost herself looking up at the enormous monarchs with tops so high they seemed to vanish.

The group halted so quickly she almost tripped over Tray. They stood at the edge of a small clearing with a fire pit in the center. The sky had grown dark with dusk, the air chilly and still.

"We sleep here," said Adven, the first time she'd heard him speak since they'd left the village. His voice had a gravelly quality, like some of the men who smoked too much of the imported tobacco leaves. "Gather wood."

"Aye, aye, sir," Cather whispered to Mayten, who swallowed a giggle. At least Cather's sense of humor was back.

Mayten winced as she slid the backpack off her shoulders and lowered it to the ground. Cather let out a small groan as she followed suit. Together they moved into the woods, filling their arms with small branches and old bark that they found lying on the ground.

Birds and squirrels scrambled and scratched overhead as the forest creatures settled for the night. The sounds quieted as the girls hunted for wood, their footsteps hushed by a thick pad of old pine needles—duff, Mayten reminded herself. Anatolian snuffled in the bushes nearby. The peace of the old-growth trees calmed her nerves and exhaustion swept over her as she breathed deeply of air that smelled of mulch and living things.

"How are your feet?" Mayten asked, keeping her voice low.

"Sore. I thought they'd fall off that last hour." Cather sighed.

"Mine too. I was worried about you. But . . . you're doing this for Tray, right? Even though the bonehead has no idea—"

Cather turned to her, her eyes shining in the growing darkness. Was she about to cry?

"I'm so sorry, Mayten. I knew you'd be devastated if I left, but I just couldn't leave Tray. I just . . . couldn't."

Mayten shifted her wood to one arm and touched Cather's shoulder with her free hand. "I know. I knew you would go if they called him . . . if you could find a way."

Cather looked at her feet for a long time, looking like she wanted to say more but didn't know how.

"What is it? What's wrong?" Mayten finally asked.

Cather glanced up. "It's . . . it's just that, well, they *had* to send you. You're the best tree singer, next to your mother. But there are lots of healers they could have sent."

What on earth did Cather mean?

"What are you saying?"

"When I heard about the trip," she spoke quickly as if to get the words out before she changed her mind, "I asked to go— begged really."

Realization tickled along Mayten's spine. "What do you mean 'when you heard about the trip?' We all heard about it at the same time, at the Leveling Ceremony."

Cather's gaze dropped again. It wasn't in her friend to lie. Mayten pictured the night before the ceremony when she'd gone to visit and how Cather had dropped her gaze while they'd visited.

"Just when did you hear about the trip, Cather?" Mayten's voice was tight with anger. Her best friend had known this was going to happen and she hadn't said a word.

Cather glanced up, peering from under her bangs. Her words came out in a flood. "My mother told me about a week before the Leveling. She'd tended a clan elder who mentioned it. Mother knew that Tray would be called to go and she knew I'd want the option to go with him, which I did. So—I spoke with the clan leader and asked Solis to send me with him."

Mayten felt . . . she wasn't certain just what she felt.

Cather rushed on. "It was the scariest moment of my life, facing that woman alone . . . and then she wouldn't give me an answer. She said I had to wait until the ceremony. I'm so sorry, Mayten . . . I didn't know for sure . . ." Her voice trailed off.

Mayten felt like something heavy had dropped on her and she couldn't get air into her lungs. "Why? Why didn't you tell me?"

"I wanted to, but Solis made me promise not to discuss it with anyone. She was furious that I knew about the trip at all and said that if I told anyone, there was no way I'd be going anywhere!"

Mayten tried to clear her mind, to think. If Cather had approached Solis, then was the clan leader's speech—"these children grew up together and are a team"—a lie? Had Mayten been added at the last minute in an attempt to make this quest sound carefully planned?

Could she be home right now if Cather hadn't begged to go?

Then what?

Would her mother be on this quest, leaving her home with the babies?

Mayten turned, anger, sadness, confusion and fatigue clouding her thoughts. "At least your mother was kind enough to let you decide if you wanted to go."

She stomped off to the firepit, dropping her armload of wood with a loud *crash!*

"Watch it, Singer!" Adven jumped as the wood tumbled near his boot. He called her "Singer" as if the word tasted bad in his mouth.

Mayten backed away from the strange man who obviously didn't want her there. Why didn't he just send her home?

Ignoring Adven's glare, she stalked to the opposite side of the clearing to gather more wood, someplace she could be alone with her thoughts.

CHAPTER NINE

The woodsman bagged a turkey large enough to feed them all and roasted it over the fire as they prepared their beds. Mayten ate with an appetite she hadn't known she had, the juicy, hot meat savory on her tongue. She carefully wiped her hands and mouth with a spare cloth when she finished, leaning against a fallen log and listening to the forest around her.

Anatolian finished his meal and plopped down beside her, laying his head in her lap. She absently stroked his soft head, glad for the lack of conversation.

Cather sat about three feet away. She yanked off her boots and applied ointments and bandages to her swollen feet. It always seemed strange that healers couldn't heal themselves using energy the same way they used it to heal others, instead having to resort to ordinary healing techniques.

Mayten almost got up to help her friend but the ring of Cather's betrayal left a bitter taste in her mouth. She focused instead on picking burrs from Anatolian's ears.

First her mother, then Cather—two people she had always trusted. Even her da had known. The deceit hit her like physical blows.

Tray sat close by, whittling away at a piece of wood with a small knife, humming tunelessly. His shaggy dark hair fell into his eyes and every few minutes he tossed his head, flipping his hair out of his eyes.

Adven shared long swigs from a waterskin with Hunter. The woodsman sat on his haunches, poking at the fire. She was certain what they drank bore no resemblance to water, though. She studied the pair while working loose the dog's burrs. Hunter looked younger than Adven, more the age of Mayten's twin sisters.

"Hunter," said Adven, his voice raised more than necessary for them all to hear, "have you no stories to relieve the monotony of this *babysitting* I must do?"

Mayten glared at their so-called leader, who insolently met her gaze. Only one eye was visible beneath his hat. She drew in a breath to tell him she'd be glad to return home but Hunter jumped to his feet, waving his arms in the air. His green eyes sparkled.

"The only thing I love more than hearing a good story," the woodsman said in an accent Mayten had never heard before, "is telling one of my own."

Then he laughed so hard he doubled over. She felt herself smiling despite her dark mood.

Firelight danced across his face as he spoke. His rust-red hair looked like tongues of flame licking up around his knitted cap. His lilting voice took on a rhythm Mayten found mesmerizing.

"Exactly eight years ago I was in these very woods, further up the great mountain. The questers were resting while I scouted for game. I'm not bragging when I say I'm the best woodsman—and hunter—in our clan. I never come back empty-handed. But there'd been a drought that year and game was hard to come by."

She'd only been seven at the time of the drought but the plants and trees had all felt the sting of thirst. Some of the clan blamed the drought for the sickness that took her siblings that winter.

"Finally, I heard something in the bush." His voice grew quiet as he crouched low and mimicked drawing a bow.

"By then I was getting desperate and perhaps a *tad* incautious." He drawled the word 'tad' and she got the sense he'd been more than a little careless.

"I tiptoed slowly toward the bush, bow ready. Then I caught the most horrible smell." He wrinkled his nose. "A smell I knew too well and should have noticed sooner. My gut clenched and I turned to run, but a great bear rose from the bush, looming over me."

The woodsman stood on his toes, arms in the air, fingers curved like claws. "He was three feet taller than I and twice as wide."

A shiver ran down Mayten's spine as he continued.

"The bear ROARED."

Mayten's heart jumped.

"Two rows of knife-sharp teeth dripped in that roaring mouth, teeth just waiting to rip me to shreds. His hot breath burned the skin of my face. Before I could run, I was knocked sideways by a blow so strong I could no longer breathe. The last thing I remember was flying through the air. I woke at the base of a tree."

The woodsman leaned closer to the fire and dropped his voice to a low whisper. "They say that when you're about to die your whole life flashes before your eyes, but that's not what happened to me. As I was flying through the air, before I hit the tree, my last thought went something like this, 'Well at least when he eats me, he'll get a mouth full of shat when he gets t' my pants!'"

Hunter slapped his thigh and doubled over, laughing hysterically. He fell onto the ground and gripped his sides. Mayten couldn't help herself; she began to laugh as well, picturing the woodsman with dirty pants and the disgusted bear.

Why was it so hard to resist laughing when someone joked about themselves? Her da was famous for that.

Cather and Tray joined in, both laughing so hard tears streamed down their cheeks. Even Adven managed a lopsided grin.

When the woodsman caught his breath, Cather asked, "But how did you get away?"

Mayten winced. Her friend was naive to believe the ridiculous story. "No one would survive a bear like that, Cather. Besides, there aren't great bears in these woods, only the smaller black ones that scare away with loud noises."

"Oh, lassie," the woodsman cooed, shaking his head. "That's where you're wrong."

He rose to one knee and turned his left side to the fire, lifting his shirt. Light from the flames shifted, causing the four white lines running up his side to dance like waves on sand.

Mayten's heart stopped. She'd seen scars like that on trees, but never with the spaces between the claws so far apart. That must have been a huge bear!

Anatolian raised his head, looking at her with concern.

"I'm okay," she whispered. "It's just a story."

Still, she couldn't resist peering at the dark trees surrounding their camp. Had something moved just beyond Adven's head?

Hunter let his shirt drop. "I'm alive today only because of this man here."

He slapped Adven on the shoulder. "If he hadn't shown up, I'd be dead or so hurt he'd have to do his duty by me. He and several other men came looking for me and lured the bear away."

"Fifteen arrows and we only managed to make him madder," Adven said. "If a boar hadn't come out of the brush and gored the injured bear, we'd have all been dead."

"What happened to the boar?" asked Tray, his words trailing off in a squeak. He scowled. She knew he was not happy at the way his voice had decided to change just when he was off on his first adventure.

"Don't know," said Adven. "We didn't stay to find out. I imagine he died rather quickly. I bet that bear is still looking for us, though." He grinned in a way that sent shivers down Mayten's back.

Hunter laughed and nodded as he sat back down by the fire. "No doubt he is."

"Uncle," Tray glanced eagerly at Adven. "Will you tell us how you lost your eye?"

Mayten glanced at the hat that dipped low over one of Adven's eyes. So that was why he wore it that way—and why he never took it off.

"Sure," said the quester. "Which version of the story do you want?"

"Well, I was hoping to hear the real one this time."

"Did you hear that, Hunter? He wants to hear the real story."

Hunter threw back his head and laughed. "Better men than you have tried to get that story from him, Tray. I wouldn't hold my breath if I were you."

Adven seemed to have had enough of their story time. He stood, brushing off his trousers. "To bed with you, children. We leave at dawn."

Mayten pulled her blanket up around her shoulders. Children indeed! That man certainly knew how to ruin a good evening.

And what if the bear story was true? How would they—how would *she*—survive this trip if they encountered a bear like that?

Cather scooted toward Mayten as if wanting close company. Mayten scowled and stood, clutching her blanket tight around her shoulders. She moved over to the closest tree, calling Anatolian to come.

A troubled look flashed across Tray's face but she didn't care. She wouldn't be as warm away from the fire, but with the tree at her back and Anatolian by her side, she wouldn't be lonely.

CHAPTER TEN

Clanging pots jarred Mayten out of a deep sleep. She groaned, blinking bleary eyes at the trees towering over her. It took a moment to remember she was on a quest and hadn't just fallen asleep among her trees. Dawn's graying skies looked almost crystalline with stars glittering here and there before fading into the growing light.

She wrinkled her nose at the acrid stench of coffee. Hunter grabbed the cook pot from the fire and poured the thick black stuff into a cup, then set the pot back on the fire. He didn't offer the younger members of their team any of the dark brew. Mayten wouldn't have accepted the awful stuff if he had. The beans had to be imported all the way from Alara, and her family drank it only at holiday time. She'd never liked the bitter taste, preferring the milder teas that arrived on ships from Caspia.

They cleaned camp, re-rolled their sleeping blankets, and ate leftover turkey Hunter had kept banked by the fire. He gave what was left of the turkey to Anatolian, who gulped it down and sniffed for more.

The dog was good at chasing and catching small chipmunks and other rodents for his meals, but Mayten was grateful that Hunter had thought to let him finish off the leftovers.

Sleeping next to the tree had lessened some of Mayten's hurt. Trees had always soothed her when emotions flared. Sleeping on hard ground, however, left her bruised and sore and scowling. Small wonder the rest of the team kept their distance.

Adven's mood didn't seem any better. He kept his hat pulled low over his eyes and barked directions at them until even Hunter seemed a bit disgruntled. Finally, Tray kicked out the fire and they were off.

The morning's walk was a repeat of the day before, Adven and Hunter in the lead, followed by Tray who seemed fascinated by every word and gesture the pair made. Cather stayed close to Tray, but Mayten held back, not wanting to talk to any of them.

She should be working with her mother, learning how to *listen*. Training to be a proper tree singer.

An array of fascinating fungi caught her attention as they went through a particularly misty section of forest, the air so damp it seemed as though the trees themselves were watering the ground. Mushrooms of every possible size, shape, and color erupted at the base of each tree.

Anatolian and Tray seemed the only ones enjoying the walk. The sound of the dog crashing through brush and splashing through nearby streams kept time with the clomp, clomp, clomping of their boots.

Morning wore on, warm sun eventually breaking through the canopy, drying moisture from both air and soil. The trees grew further and further apart and they found themselves walking through an arid section almost barren of trees. A closer look showed that a fire had swept through the area recently. Dust tickled Mayten's nose and clogged her throat. She was parched and tired but refused to ask for a break.

On they went, trekking up and down hills, on and on and on until even the trees looked the same.

When the sun beat straight down on them and Mayten thought she couldn't take another step, they stopped for lunch.

Cather and Mayten went off into the bushes to relieve themselves while the men did the same in another direction. Anatolian searched the bushes for his lunch.

"I can't stand this anymore," Cather said as they headed back to the others. "Can't stand you shutting me out like this. I told you I was sorry. What more do you want?"

What she wanted was to be left alone, but Mayten didn't say that. She forced herself to take a moment, to understand why she was so angry.

"It just surprised me," she finally said. "I felt so foolish. Like everyone knew except me."

She stopped and turned to her friend. "Don't you think my mom could have told me?" The words tumbled out. "She knew before anyone else. Why didn't she . . . I just felt so stupid up there on that stage. It was like . . . like getting hit from behind."

Cather's lip quivered. Before she could say anything, shouts rang out up ahead.

"Tray, quick, climb the tree. It's a wild boar." Mayten recognized Hunter's voice.

"Tray's in trouble." Cather darted ahead.

Straight toward the commotion.

"Cather, stop," Mayten called, running after her. Cather was a clan dweller. She didn't know the things a homesteader knew, didn't know a boar could rip you apart with their sharp curved tusks.

As they drew near, Cather stopped. Mayten grabbed her from behind and held her tight.

"The men are there. They'll help Tray. There's nothing we can do."

Mayten slammed sideways as Anatolian rushed toward the ruckus.

"Anatolian, come back!" Panic seized her in a stranglehold. A dog was no match for a boar!

A tree about ten feet ahead swayed violently. She couldn't see the boar through the thick brush.

But she could see the tree's branches.

"Look!" She pointed about a third of the way up the tree. "Tray's safe."

Tray looked terrified, clinging to the thick branches, his eyes tightly closed.

"Help, help," he yelled. "Get it away from me!"

Anatolian barked and the tree shook violently. Mayten held Cather back, forcing her to crouch behind a bush that smelled strangely pungent. She couldn't see her dog, but he sounded more excited than threatened.

Where was Adven? And where had Hunter gone?

She bit her lip and looked around for something to throw. If the men weren't going to help Tray, it was up to her and Cather.

She needed something to get the boar's attention.

Mayten refused to think about what would happen once she got that attention. They'd likely end up in a tree, like Tray.

Better than walking . . .

The thought almost made her giggle.

She finally found what she was looking for—a branch as thick as Oleaster's arm. She snatched up the branch . . .

And paused.

How many times had Da told her that boars weren't opportunistic attackers? They would avoid you if they could and attack if you got between them and their piglets.

But they didn't stalk people.

She put her finger to her lips and beckoned to Cather. They crept closer and Mayten pushed aside the bush's thorny branches.

Adven crouched at the base of the tree, rocking the trunk with his shoulder while Hunter crouched close by, making loud snuffling noises. Anatolian jumped around them, barking with glee.

"What are they . . ." Cather's voice trailed off as she realized what was happening. She jumped to her feet.

"Stop that," she screamed. "Stop it right now!"

The men looked at each other and burst out laughing. Adven sank back on his heels and Anatolian sniffed him, then started licking the man's face.

Adven shoved the dog away, scrubbing at his face with his sleeve. Cather stomped up to the men, fists planted on her hips, looking as though she might punch one of them.

"Tray, come down," Mayten called. "There is no boar."

He opened his eyes and looked down at the men still chuckling. He carefully climbed down the tree until he could jump to the ground. He glared at his uncle with fists clenched.

"That wasn't funny," he said, his jaw tight.

Hunter gave Cather a cautious glance before turning to Tray. "Come on, think about it. Would we let a boar send you up a tree like that? It was pretty funny."

Tray stood perfectly still for a long moment. Then his frown turned to a grin. A chortle escaped his lips and soon he was laughing just as hard as the other two. The men slapped his shoulders, mimicking his panicked screams.

Mayten shook her head in disgust as she pulled Cather away. If *she'd* been the one up the tree, she'd be furious. "Men. I'll never understand them."

Cather looked like she'd been the one chased by the boar. She took a deep breath and rubbed at her chest. "I was so scared, Mayten. What would I do if . . . I've never told him how I feel."

Mayten put an arm around her friend and felt her own heart rate slow. "They ever try that on me, somebody's gonna die."

To her surprise, Cather giggled. "I'll be sure and stay out of the way."

Hunter yelled that it was time to go and they fell back into line. The men continued to laugh and joke as they walked and Cather and Mayten brought up the rear.

It felt right to have Cather at her side. She'd missed the closeness the two of them had shared ever since they were small.

"I know Adven wants to get to the castle as soon as possible, but I'm never going to get a chance to listen to the trees if he keeps this up." Mayten didn't realize she was thinking out loud until Cather made a sympathetic sound.

"All this walking leaves me so tired I can't think," Cather agreed.

For as long as she could remember, Mayten had been taught that all living things had energy running through them. A singer's job was to align the energy within their own bodies with the living thing they were supposed to be helping: trees, flowers, or, in Taiwania's case, the clan's communal history and spirit. That was why singers like her sister made good clan leaders— they could *feel* the clan.

Mayten had never tried to connect with a tree's energy from a distance. *Might be good practice. Who knows if I'll get a chance to do it right?*

So she tried. As she walked, she took her love for all living things, shut out all distractions (a Level Two training), and focused her eyes on the path about three feet ahead of her. Didn't want to trip on any roots.

Then she blocked out everything else—the banter of the men, the birdsong, the squish of pine needles under her boots, the sound of Anatolian rummaging in the bush . . .

Focusing on one tree as she walked wasn't feasible so she decided to just talk, but in her mind, not out loud. Verbal communication was a Level Three skill, one she excelled at. But she'd never tried to communicate mentally.

:*Hello friends,*: she sent. :*I'm trying to learn about the blight in the land. I want to help, but I don't know what to do. Can you help? Can you tell me anything?*:

Then she fell quiet, struggling to keep quiet, to move into Level Four, listening.

For a long time, she heard nothing at all. Just as she was about to give up, Mayten swore she heard what she could only describe as—giggles.

The joy of the wind in the branches, she realized. The realization expanded, opening her to the tickle of squirrels dancing along the limbs and the urgency of baby birds chirping in their nests. The communal happiness of spring . . .

Emotions surged through her, cleansing the rest of her foul mood from the night before and the boar prank, washing away everything but the hope of the trees.

I made a connection! Elation filled Mayten's soul. *Just wait until I tell Mother . . .*

Anger settled back over her like a damp cloak and she lost her focus, lost the connection.

She tried to push the anger away, regain her focus. If she tried hard enough, there was a chance she could also receive visual messages, a Level Five skill—

"Hello, Mayten." Hunter's voice made her jump. How long had he been walking beside her?

"Hi," she said tentatively. Whatever did the woodsman want? She glanced up to see Cather had moved up alongside Tray as the path had broadened. Adven maintained his position as head of the team . . . with Anatolian at his heels.

"Sorry if our little prank scared you." Hunter sounded sincere.

"Cather's the one you should apologize to." Mayten jerked her chin at her friend. "I think you took a few years off her life."

"Already did," he said. They walked quietly together for a bit.

"Do you know that I was in the same leveling class as Acerola and Zigba?"

The question surprised Mayten. She didn't remember seeing Hunter around while the twins were in training. "You were?"

Two days away from home and she was already homesick, Mayten realized. How sweet of him to bring up her sisters.

"Yep, and I've got a story to tell you!" His eyes sparkled as he waggled his eyebrows.

She liked Hunter, Mayten decided. Not only had he been kind to Anatolian, he'd also been thoughtful enough to apologize. He was almost the opposite of Adven. Their team *leader* would never think to apologize to anyone or check on how they were doing.

Anatolian waited beside a tree as they passed. He moved up next to Hunter and pressed against his side. The woodsman stroked the dog's broad head as they walked.

"Those sisters of yours used to pretend each was the opposite twin all the time, like it was their private little joke."

Mayten laughed. "They did that at home, but I didn't know they did it anywhere else."

His eyes twinkled. "I could always tell them apart. Because Zigba has the smallest scar right by her lip."

Mayten nodded. She used that little scar to tell them apart, too. Zigba had fallen from a tree and cut her lip on a rock. But Zigba's scar was tiny and Mayten was surprised Hunter had noticed it.

"It was the solstice celebration," he continued, "and I knew those girls were up to something. I'd been watching them, you see. There was this boy in the clan who was intent on courting Zigba. I knew he planned to get her attention at the dance. Well, the girls snuck off and I followed them. They traded hair scarves where no one could see. 'Twas the only way to tell them apart that day."

"Oh my." Mayten giggled, picturing her sisters doing just that.

"Just to make life interesting, I told the boy who was interested in Zigba what they had done. He went up and asked Acerola, pretending to be Zigba, to dance. At the end of the dance, he made sure to stop before the real Zigba and kissed Acerola—right in front of her sister!"

Hunter chuckled and Mayten found herself joining him. She'd have to remember to tease her sisters about that one when she got back.

"What did Acerola do?"

"She sputtered, turned a most satisfying shade of red, and stomped off the dance floor, Zigba running after her." His wistful smile made Mayten wonder if there was more to the story than he was telling. She studied his freckles for a long moment.

"Hunter, can I ask you something kind of personal?"

"You can ask me anything, anytime, lassie," Hunter tipped his hat, encouraging her to go on.

"It's just, your skin is so . . ."

"White?"

"Yes," she said with a rush of relief. "And red. And those freckles . . ."

"Simple," he said with a grin. "My da was from the green Isle of Ister. He came over on a trading ship and fell in love with a girl from the Ocean Clan. Lots of people from Ister have red hair and white skin with freckles. He took me once to see the Old Land, as he calls it. My skin is actually darker than most, because of my ma. You should see how pale my da is! Scare ya to death!"

Mayten laughed, surprised to find Hunter so easy to talk to. "So how did you end up here?"

"I wasn't meant for the sea, threw up all the way to Ister and back. And I had no gift with my hands, but I was always great with a bow. I begged to be apprenticed to a woodsman and finally my da gave in. They sent me over to your clan where I started my training a bit late. When I got the blank apron, I asked if I could try hunting for a questing team and the rest, as they say, is history!"

CHAPTER ELEVEN

That night after dinner they sat around the fire near an aspen grove. Mayten rubbed her sore feet and tried to stretch out her aching back.

Adven turned to Cather. "All right, Healer. What stories do you have?"

Tray perked up and Hunter added a couple more sticks to the fire. Anatolian was curled up around Mayten's feet.

Cather straightened her back and smiled shyly. "Healers don't have stories like you do. We don't get chased by wild beasts, but I have heard stories of the strange things healers have seen."

"Like what?" Tray asked, leaning toward her.

Cather smiled, setting her dimples dancing.

If that boy can't see how gorgeous she is, he's blind. Mayten *almost* rolled her eyes.

"Like the time one of the tree cutters got his leg crushed under a tree that fell the wrong way. My great-aunt said his leg had been crushed and there was nothing they could do to fix it. They had to cut the poor man's leg off with a tree saw."

Mayten shivered. No one in her clan had one leg, not in her memory anyway. Had the tree cutter died?

"Old Gimpy." Adven nodded. "I remember him."

"Yes," Cather agreed. "He died when I was a baby, but one of the carpenters fashioned a half leg made of wood for him and I guess he lived many years after the accident."

Mayten swallowed hard, studying her friend a bit more closely. How could Cather be so casual about something so awful? She would certainly not want to spend her life cutting off limbs.

"Cather, what's the strangest thing you've ever seen?" Tray asked. "With your own eyes, I mean."

It was so dark that Mayten could barely see Tray on the far side of the fire. Firelight flickered across his face, chest, and knees, but all else was lost in the blackness that pressed close all around.

Cather didn't hesitate. "That one is easy. We were delivering Lizzy Builder's baby and after we'd delivered a precious little girl, Lizzy started heaving again."

Mayten knew this story by heart. Her friend had raced up the mountain that day, excited to tell her about the special birth.

"Then we delivered a little boy," Cather continued. "He was beautiful too. We were getting him all cleaned up when Lizzy started heaving again. This time she gave birth to a second boy, a tiny little thing. He wasn't formed right. It looked as though his spine hadn't closed up in the back. He never even took a breath. It was the saddest thing." Her face mirrored the sorrow in her words. "I'd never heard of three babies born at once. I only wish he'd lived."

"I never heard of such a thing either," Tray said.

"Wouldn't have believed it if I hadn't held him in my own hands," Cather said in a distant voice.

Mayten knew her friend wasn't sitting around the campfire right then. She was back with Lizzy, holding the tiny stillborn baby.

Adven cleared his throat. "What kinds of tales do singers have? Do they *sing* to each other every night?" He laughed—at least she thought it was a laugh. Sounded more like rocks rubbing together.

What had she done to make this man hate her so?

The joy she'd felt moments ago vanished as she took a breath, determined not to let him see her confusion. "No, we don't sing to each other. Our stories are more . . . informational than sensational."

"Tell us one," Tray said. He sounded overly enthusiastic, like he was trying to make up for his uncle's rudeness.

A log shifted on the fire, sending sparks dancing into the night sky. Smoke stung Mayten's nose as she considered the stories she knew.

"Once, a long time ago," she began, "a trading ship came to Trigginsfeld bearing a cargo of eucalyptus saplings. This happened back when the clan was young and just starting to build. There were already pine forests and an oak woodland, but the people wanted to build fast without stripping the forest. The ship's trader claimed the trees would grow to a man's height or more every year. The people were thrilled. They bought all the saplings and planted them among the oaks. The trees matured quickly just as the man said, but they grew with scrawny, twisted trunks useless for building."

"That's what happens when you *plant* something where it doesn't belong," Adven said.

Mayten's face flamed hot as the fire. "Those eucalyptus trees are useful in many ways."

"Healers use the oil from the leaves for all kinds of things!" Cather chimed in.

"Well," Adven grumbled. "Wasn't that—educational. Time for bed, children. Get some sleep and don't give me a hard time when morning comes early."

Mayten grimaced. The man was a grouch, among other things. She laid out her blanket near the fire as the nights were chilly. Cather joined her, pulling her own blanket over them both. Anatolian stretched out on Mayten's other side, making her feel warm and secure.

The crackling fire was peaceful but sleep was a long time coming despite her exhaustion. Mayten couldn't get the sting of Adven's words out of her skull.

Cather wasn't sleeping either. She must know how Adven's words hurt. She put her hand on Mayten's shoulder and leaned close. "Aye-aye, Captain."

Mayten smiled, grateful to have at least one person who understood. She pulled Wollemi's star rock from her pocket and rubbed it between her fingers, knowing he slept under the same stars.

Was he thinking of her while he gazed at his stars?

She looked at the stars, missing her little brother so much it hurt. "I love you, Wollemi," she whispered. "I wish I was home with you."

�♫

Their days fell into a pattern. They rose early, ate leftovers from the night before—and walked. They ate a lot of meat, which was unusual for Mayten. Her family ate an abundance of vegetables, nuts, and fruit, saving meat for special occasions.

Every day their group walked until Mayten thought she would drop. Most of the time, the men stayed ahead, followed by Mayten and Cather. Sometimes Adven would stop, sniff at the air, and bend to look at the ground before continuing.

Sometimes Tray or Hunter would drop back to talk. Mayten enjoyed chatting with Hunter. He always seemed the perfect contrast to Adven's surly disposition. How on earth had the two ever become friends?

The woodsman had no end of stories to tell, making time pass more quickly. He seemed to enjoy spending time with Mayten, spinning stories about her sisters Mayten had never heard.

Anatolian roamed around the group as they traveled. The big dog had no trouble keeping himself fed on ground squirrels and other small creatures he flushed from the bushes and trees.

Hunter not only brought in meat for their supper, he knew which plants were good to eat, digging mushrooms and roots to add to whatever game filled the small pot he carried in his pack. Mayten often joined him in his search for greens, putting some of her lesser training to use.

After dinner and storytelling, they went to sleep early and slept hard.

She had little time to listen to the trees.

On their fourth day away from home the weather turned warm, leaving Mayten's skin sticky and moist. The forest of spruce, fir, and pine trees was filled with a musky odor and rang with birdsong, seeming magical in the dusky morning light. The path squished under her boots, feeling more like wet cloth than dirt.

Anatolian didn't seem inclined to stray in the damp heat, trotting along with his tongue lolling out one side of his mouth.

Tray dropped back and walked quietly beside Anatolian. Mayten gave him a welcoming smile. She always enjoyed talking with her friend. She missed him. He also knew more about what was happening than the girls did. Cather was ahead talking to Hunter so Mayten had Tray to herself for a change.

"Any idea how far we are from the king's castle?" she asked.

Tray shrugged. "Adven says we should be there within three days if all goes well."

Mayten felt as though a tree had been lifted off her shoulders. Finally—an end to all this walking. She glanced at her friend and cleared her throat. There was something that had been niggling at the back of her mind and he might be able to help.

"Do you remember that first night when Hunter told us that story about the bear?"

"Yeah."

"He said something I've been puzzling about. When the bear hit him and he thought he was going to die or be badly hurt, he said, 'Adven would have had to do his duty by me.' What did he mean?"

Tray fell silent as they walked. "You know how each calling has codes," he finally said. "Rules of behavior that are important for the safety of the members."

Mayten nodded. Singers had to be aware of their surroundings. There were hazards to be avoided in the trees and bushes, like snakes or certain spiders or poisonous frogs. Singers were trained to watch out for those as well as plants that could sting or cause rashes.

Tray smiled at her. Then his smile faded. "Questers also have a code. About extreme situations. If someone gets hurt— really, really hurt, not just a little—and that person won't be able to continue the quest . . . if there is no way to get that person home . . . we won't leave them to die alone."

"So you stay with them out here in the forest," Mayten said, her voice disbelieving. "Until they die?"

She couldn't . . . *wouldn't* . . . believe it. No one would just let a friend die.

"Not exactly," Tray said. He sounded . . . uncertain. "It's part of a Questor's code. We can't delay the quest for more than two days, and it's dangerous for anyone to be left alone when the one who's hurt dies, so . . ."

"I don't understand," Mayten said. She struggled with Tray's words. If you couldn't help a person who was dying . . .

Ice water ran down her spine.

"You kill them?" she shouted.

"Shhh," Tray cautioned. "We're not supposed to talk about it, and I don't think it happens very often. But you have to understand—it's our duty to help the person pass easily."

"What do you mean 'easily'?" Mayten felt her throat tighten. What if that someone was Tray or Cather? How could she help *them* die?

"There are ways. It's part of our training."

As if that made everything clear as water in spring.

They walked in silence for a long time, each lost in their own thoughts.

Did other callings have those kinds of secrets?

CHAPTER TWELVE

The next day, the weather took a definite turn. Wind whipped the tops of the pines and icy air bit into Mayten's skin. Mayten quickly rolled her blanket and repacked her things, shivering as she shouldered her pack and joined the others. Cather looked as cold as Mayten felt as they pulled on tightly knitted woolen rain ponchos and caps.

Only Anatolian and Adven seemed unaffected by the weather change. The grin on Anatolian's furry face made Mayten's heart a little lighter.

A light mist fell, bringing the colors of the forest alive as the summer's dust washed away.

She didn't know the name of the trees covered completely in lime green moss. She thought of them as Light Seekers. Resplendent in their green coats, the trees shot up between thick, straight pines, arching over the trail as they sought the sun.

Enormous ferns as big as Anatolian and larger, carpeted the hillsides in darker greens, surrounded by clover sporting yet another greenish hue. It was as if the forest had been painted by a magic fairy with a pallet of greens.

Wind whipped the trees overhead as the mist thickened into rain, but Mayten was so caught up in the beauty of their surroundings she didn't care.

She paused beside a Light Seeker. Up close, the tree looked to be wearing a coat made of tiny ferns instead of moss. She ran a finger over the tree's velvety coat, listening for the tree's voice—

Bam!

Pain exploded through Mayten's head. Though she didn't remember falling, she found herself flat on her back, staring up into Cather's face, feeling her friend's hot hands on her neck. Her skull felt as though someone had split it in two.

"What . . . ?" She tried to sit up, but someone had her shoulders pinned to the ground.

"Wait, Mayten, hold still." Tray's quiet voice near her ear calmed her galloping heart. Somewhere close by Anatolian whined.

Cather's eyes were closed, her forehead furrowed in concentration. Rain streamed off strands of her wet hair; her woolen cap was not much help as the rain increased. Tray bent over Mayten's shoulder, his wide-brimmed hat shielding her from the rain, but Cather wasn't so lucky.

The pain increased until Mayten swore her head would explode like a rotten pumpkin dropped from a roof. She tried again to sit up, but Tray's grip was firm.

A feeling of peace and wellness flooded over her, sweeping the pain away and leaving her exhausted but whole. Cather opened her eyes, concern clearly showing in their brown depths.

Anatolian licked Mayten's face as Tray released her shoulders. Together, Tray and Cather helped Mayten sit. It took a few breaths before the world stopped spinning.

"What happened?" Mayten finally asked. Anatolian forced himself as far into her lap as he could fit and plopped down, gazing up at her with deep brown eyes.

She ruffled his fur and gently pushed his head—and his stinky breath—away from her face.

Tray leaned down and held up a pinecone at least two feet long and as thick as a log.

"You got knocked on the head by one of those . . ." Cather pointed. "It could have broken your neck. Thankfully, you ended up with nothing more than a hard bump on the head and I could heal it."

"Are we ready to move on?" Adven called.

Hunter and Adven waited further up the trail, Hunter looking worried, Adven looking . . . like Adven, grumpy and impatient.

Cather raised an eyebrow in question.

"I'm fine," Mayten said. Couldn't he at least give her a moment to gather her sense? "Let's go."

Tray and Cather pulled her to her feet as she tried to brush muddy paw prints off her pants. Tray handed Mayten her pack and she shrugged it back on, taking a moment to remove her cap and rub her head. Her hair was wet, but her skull felt smooth. She could find no sign of a bump. An odd sensation swept over her, leaving her dizzy and slightly disoriented.

Was this what it was like to be healed? Having a memory of the injury but no injury itself?

Mayten had probably been healed as a child—most children suffer an illness or injury that would require a healer—but she couldn't remember being healed. Healers weren't bothered with everyday colds or scratches and she'd always been pretty healthy. .

Adven stomped off, Hunter close on his heels, though the woodsman glanced over his shoulder several times as if reassuring himself she was following.

Cather stayed beside Mayten, matching her pace, casting glances at her now and again.

Mayten fastened the top of her cape close around her throat as the wind hurled another rain-laden gust against them. Questions chased each other through her mind, like squirrels in spring.

"When you healed me," she finally asked Cather. "Your hands felt hot, almost burning, on my neck. Then this feeling of peace came over me. Is that what usually happens?"

Cather shrugged. "That's what I hear."

"What does it feel like to you? Do your hands burn? Did you feel my pain?"

Why had she never thought to ask this before? As close as their friendship was, they had never shared much about their training. There were other things they wanted to do and there was always so little time.

Cather looked thoughtful, and Mayten gave her time to think. Icy rain snaked along Mayten's scalp and trickled down her back, sending shivers down her arms. The wool was starting to smell funny but continued to keep her top half fairly dry. Her legs, however, were soaked to the skin and her feet were sloshing in her boots.

"It's like I close my eyes and open my heart to the energy all around us," Cather said with a nod. "Then I sort of scan the body of the person I'm helping, looking—or feeling—for places where the flow of energy has been interrupted or is too loud or too soft. Does that make sense?"

"It's like how we can sense the energy flowing through a tree and sort of help shape its growth." Mayten wiped at the rain trickling down her face.

"Exactly," Cather said, "and if there is an injury, I can give my energy to that place, help it heal more quickly. From what I understand, this is how most healers work."

Mayten frowned. "But when I help a tree, it gives back to me. It's like we're working in partnership. Is that how it works when someone is hurt? Do they give energy back to you?"

"No, they can't." Cather's foot caught a root, and she pitched forward. Mayten grabbed her arm to keep her from falling. The wind drove the rain directly in their faces, making it increasingly difficult to see.

Cather smiled her thanks before continuing. "It actually drains the energy from me. I have to rest, drink water, and eat more to recover."

"I didn't realize," Mayten said, finally understanding why her friend always had such a big appetite but never gained weight. She eyed Cather in dismay. Grumpy Adven hadn't even given her friend time to recuperate. No wonder she was tripping over roots. "Thank you. Thank you for healing me *and* for giving me your energy."

Cather laughed, making her dimples dance. "That didn't take much. A bump on the head is pretty basic and doesn't take a lot of energy. There are more complicated types of healing, injuries I don't know how to heal yet, that take almost everything a healer can give. Some injuries—and some diseases—are so bad no one can heal them, no matter how experienced the healer might be."

Mayten was sure Cather was being modest. Her friend was an excellent student and her parents were very respected healers. She'd spent her entire life helping with healings.

"What about that peaceful feeling—"

"Whoa!" Hunter put out his hand, stopping Mayten before she walked right into him. Both she and Cather had been walking with their heads down, trying to keep the rain from their faces. They hadn't noticed the men coming back towards them.

"We have to rope up," said Hunter. "The trail narrows around the bend and the water is starting to wash parts of it away."

Mayten looked around. The rain came down in sheets and water puddled on the trail. Anatolian looked miserable but continued slapping her legs with his wet tail.

Adven had already tied a rope around his waist. He let out four feet of rope and tied it around Tray. Mayten's hands were stiff with cold. She wondered how he could even tie the rope. He did the same with Cather, then Mayten, roping Hunter last. Without saying a word, Adven turned and lead the way forward, Anatolian bounding ahead of him.

Mayten was surprised at how slippery the trail had become. The trail dirt was the consistency of mud that was both clingy and slippery. She focused on staying on her feet, rubbing her hands and tucking them under her arms in an attempt to stay warm. Conversation was impossible.

They rounded the bend and the trail began to narrow as Hunter had warned. They were single file now, four feet apart on the narrow cliff trail. The mountain rose steeply on one side of the trail and dropped just as abruptly off the far side. Rivulets washed down the hillside and swept across the trail, disappearing over the cliff.

This is why trained questers are needed. Questers were trained to handle these kinds of situations. Despite his grumpy attitude, Mayten felt a grudging respect for Adven. He'd kept them safe—so far.

The trail angled upward as the wind roared through the tops of the trees, sending pinecones crashing to the ground and driving needles and rain into their faces. Mayten found herself flinching when pinecones thudded nearby and walked with her arms over her head. This would not be an easy spot to try and heal someone.

She dared a quick look over the edge, spotting a stream far below that quickly turned into a rushing river.

Shouldn't they be finding some sort of cover from the storm instead of slogging on through it? Even Anatolian looked miserable, walking with his head down, rain dripping from his sodden fur.

Mayten tightened her jaw. Maybe Adven wasn't as knowledgeable as he acted. Why wouldn't he let them stop? Why keep on moving when simply walking was becoming more and more dangerous?

She opened her mouth to call out to Adven. She would insist they stop—

Her body jerked forward just as Cather disappeared.

CHAPTER THIRTEEN

The rope jerked Mayten off her feet onto her rear and dragged her toward a gaping gash where the trail had once been. She kicked and dug with her hands and feet, trying to find something to brace against or grab hold of. Anatolian barked frantically, running back and forth on the narrow path. The dog had been trotting ahead of the group and was unable to get to her, looking as helpless as she felt.

She saw Tray clinging to the root of a tree that jutted out from the hillside across the gap from her, Adven's arms tight around his waist. Then she felt Hunter grab her pack from behind and her slide forward stopped two feet from the gap. Cather's weight pulled at Mayten, stealing her breath and hurting her ribs.

"Get Cather!" Mayten demanded. The rope was cutting her in two, but she didn't dare move. Cather was the weight on that rope. She didn't know how Hunter was still holding her, but she was grateful.

They had to get to Cather. Images of her friend—scared and possibly hurt—dangling over the chasm caused her heart to pound wildly. Not many people knew it, but Cather was afraid of heights. She must be petrified.

Slowly, Adven inched around Tray, who seemed to have a good grip on the tree root above him. Adven bent down to look over the rim of the collapsed path.

"Mayten, stand up," he ordered. "Hunter, help her."

Fear clenched at Mayten's stomach. What if Hunter let go? Would she slide right over the edge after Cather, pulling everyone after her?

But she had to move. Had to help get Cather safe.

She felt Hunter's hands move around her stomach. He gripped the rope around her waist and helped her get her legs under her. Slowly, she strained against the rope, forcing her knees to straighten until she was standing.

"Cather, give me your hand," Adven shouted over the sound of the rain. He reached down as Hunter helped Mayten creep backward, tightening the rope. Rain pounded her head, her shoulders. Her boots slipped, then held, then slipped again.

Just when she thought they'd never get Cather back, a wool hat rose through the gap. Relief washed over Mayten. Cather's hand waved in the air, then clutched at Adven's wrist. Slow as a snail in winter, Cather's shoulders rose into sight. The rope that had been around her waist had slipped up under her arms.

It almost slid right off! Mayten shivered. Adven beckoned to Mayten who took a careful step forward, then another. Adven pulled on the rope and Cather at the same time, dragging her the rest of the way onto solid ground and then moving around Tray to the front of the line.

Tray stepped forward and wrapped Cather's shaking body in a tight hug. Mayten could hear Cather sobbing over the driving rain.

Along with a nearly overwhelming sense of relief came boiling anger.

If Adven hadn't been in such a hurry, her friend would not have fallen off a cliff and almost died. There was a difference between moving fast and being foolhardy.

Their grand leader beckoned to Mayten and Hunter. Did he expect them to jump over that gap?

"It's not as wide as it seems," Hunter murmured in her ear. "And I'll be right here behind you."

She took a deep breath, tried to calm her wild heart. What if she jumped and the rest of the trail gave way?

Anatolian whined and Hunter urged her on. She took a few steps back and then two running steps forward and jumped, releasing her breath as her feet landed on solid ground, Hunter hopping easily after her.

Adven gave a quick nod, then continued along the trail, the rope pulling Tray away from Cather and forcing them onward. The trail sloped downward, leading them toward the other side of the canyon.

Mayten kept her eyes glued to the path ahead, paranoid she might slip again. The path widened and became rockier as they went down into a valley filled with oaks and maples. Anatolian dropped back beside her, pressing against her leg as they walked.

Mayten's anger simmered as they half-walked and half-slid down the stony trail. She couldn't seem to get Adven's snide looks and nasty remarks out of her head.

And she couldn't get over the way he pushed them relentlessly forward, disregarding their safety and almost getting her best friend killed.

Eventually, they reached the valley floor and Adven led them under a large stand of oaks out of the wind and rain. The nearby river raged and rushed, tumbling an occasional rock downstream.

Adven untied his end of the rope and told them to set up camp. Calm and unfeeling as though no one had almost died.

Mayten's fingers trembled as she untied the rope around her waist. Her head had stopped hurting but anger was building up inside like a thunderstorm. She stalked up to Adven, hands on her hips.

"I thought you were supposed to be the best quester around," she snarled. "Even I could see it was getting dangerous to keep walking. We should have stopped hours ago."

Adven glared down at her, arms crossed over his chest. His face was like stone but his one good eye radiated hatred.

Cather took her arm while Tray stepped up to her other side. Together, they turned her away from Adven, walking her in the opposite direction. Hunter muttered something to Adven but was shrugged off.

"I'm okay," Cather said in a soothing voice. "I'm okay."

She put her arm around Mayten's shoulders. Tray gave her an awkward pat as they scanned the forest for firewood. Not that they'd find any wood dry enough to burn in all this rain.

"Adven knows what he's doing, Mayten," Cather said. "If we hadn't been roped, I'd be gone right now."

"We shouldn't have been on that cliff in the rain." Mayten stared at her friend in disbelief. How could she defend that—

"It was a hard call," Tray said. "If we'd waited, the whole trail could have washed out. It might have taken days to find a way around. Can't you see how bad he feels about it?"

"No, I can't," said Mayten. She tucked her hands under her arms, trying to stop their trembling. "As far as I can see, the man has no feelings at all."

Tray turned and walked away, shaking his head. Cather started to follow.

"Are you really okay?" Mayten stopped Cather with a hand on her arm.

"I'm really okay." Cather rubbed at her ribs. "Just a little sore from the rope, that's all."

A twinge pierced Mayten's side where the rope had cut into her as she pulled Cather into a hug. "I'm so sorry. I know how scared you must have been." She reluctantly let her friend go, feeling a little of her tension ease. "I just wish I could heal you like you did me."

"Hey," Cather said with a grin. "You got bonked on the head and I got rope burns. If that's the worst that happens, then I imagine we're having a pretty good quest! "

CHAPTER FOURTEEN

T he storm passed as night wore on and they were up and moving before first light. Everything was soaked and no one had slept well. Adven ignored Mayten and she did her best to ignore him. According to Hunter, they'd lost a half day struggling through the storm and Adven was bent on pushing them to make up for it.

The part of the forest they found themselves in was almost abnormally quiet, with dappled sunlight filtering through the leafy oaks, casting a magical feel to the air. She'd loved reading about fairies when she was young and this seemed a perfect place for a fairytale. A light mist filled the air.

Feels more like we're walking through a painting rather than on a well-traveled trail, she mused.

A noise to her right caught her attention. A ray of sunlight fell on a small herd of deer standing in the trees. The deer startled, some of them bolting just as a small doe dropped to the ground, an arrow through its eye.

Hunter walked up to the downed doe and retrieved his arrow. Mayten watched in shock as he and Adven strung a rope and hung the doe by her heels. She turned away when Hunter brought out his long hunting knife.

She hadn't even seen him shoot.

Her heart squeezed as she watched the last of the herd crashing through the brush and trees. She enjoyed eating the meals that the woodsman cooked, but she had never witnessed a kill. Her family traded what they grew for already dressed meat.

Anatolian ran over, sniffing noisily while Hunter worked. Bile burned Mayten's throat as she watched the woodsman gutting the deer and throwing the innards to the dog. Much as she loved Anatolian, sometimes his eating habits were downright disgusting.

She imagined Adven would have no trouble slitting her throat if she got badly hurt. He would likely enjoy that task.

Adven's gravelly voice broke into her thoughts.

"Tray, take the girls on ahead. I'll stay and help Hunter. We'll catch up with you. We need to keep moving as long as we have daylight."

Cather walked up, looking as green as Mayten felt. They walked in silence as Tray led them away from the grizzly scene. Humidity from the previous night's storm made her damp clothes feel clammy against her skin. She whistled for her dog to join them.

They'd been walking about ten minutes when a scream echoed off the trees, sending fear down Mayten's spine. Anatolian took off at a run, heading back along the trail.

"Anatolian, come back!" Mayten shouted.

The girls turned to Tray, whose face had gone white as fresh-washed linen.

"Maybe they're just pranking you again," Mayten said.

Tray shook his head. "That wasn't a human scream. That was a mountain lion."

He pulled the hunting knife strapped to his leg, checked the blade, and slid the knife back in its sheath, then dashed after Anatolian.

Mayten's heart leaped to her throat. She grabbed Cather's hand and followed Tray, breaking into a run after a few steps. Shouting and barking filled the air, pierced now and again by that awful, blood-freezing scream.

"Do you think this is real?" Mayten gasped as they approached the last bend. "I wouldn't put it past Adven to pull another joke."

Cather shrugged. "We won't know unless we look."

The first thing Mayten saw when they rounded the bend was Hunter crumpled unmoving on the ground. Anatolian's teeth were fastened on the throat of the biggest cat she had ever seen. The enormous cat thrashed about, flinging Anatolian left and right like a child's doll as it tried to get free.

Tray and Adven stabbed at the cat with knives—knives!—and iron tang of blood filled the air. They missed more than they hit, dodging out of the way as the cat flung Anatolian one way, then the other. Blood was everywhere. Mayten couldn't tell whether the blood came from the cat, her dog, or Hunter, who still hadn't moved.

Anatolian—somehow—managed to pin the flailing cat on its back. Adven darted in, sinking his long hunting knife into the cat's stomach and yanking it downward, spilling entrails across the ground. The cat screamed as Adven lifted his knife and drove it home once again.

The cat went still.

The stench of death filled Mayten's nose and throat. She stumbled to the bushes and fell to her knees, ridding her stomach of breakfast. The cat's final moments played over and over again in her mind, prompting another round of heaving. She shook from head to toe, wanting nothing more than to roll into a ball and hide.

When she could finally stand, Mayten turned, intending to ask what she could do to help. But her knees went weak and wobbly at the sight before her. The deer carcass lay in pieces and a few feet away lay the mutilated mountain lion, its paws the size of a man's spread hand.

A few feet from the cat, Tray kneeled next to Adven, who sat—alive but pale and exhausted—propped against a tree.

Hunter hadn't moved. Anatolian lay against the woodsman's side, blood-splattered and weary, watching as Cather leaned over the woodsman. Her pack lay open beside her. With swift efficiency, Cather looked in Hunter's eyes and felt his pulse. Then she closed her eyes and rested her hands on Hunter's chest.

She hadn't raced for the bushes and puked up her guts. She'd gotten to work.

This is her calling, Mayten reminded herself.

But that didn't take away Mayten's feeling of helplessness. The ability to communicate with trees was no help at all in a situation like this.

Was that why Adven resented her?

She took a step toward Anatolian and Hunter, grateful her legs didn't wobble. She'd check Anatolian out. Make sure he wasn't hurt—

"But he's a woodsman," Tray said, his voice tight with pain. "He would have felt the cat's presence."

"He was distracted," Adven said.

Mayten glanced their way, startled by the venom in Adven's voice. His good eye glared at her as he shoved Tray aside and struggled to his feet. He seemed to be in one piece, though she didn't know if the blood on his clothing was his, Hunter's, or the mountain lion's.

"The cat took us by surprise," he said to no one in particular. He moved around the clearing, picking up the contents of a scattered pack. "Jumped right on Hunter, grabbed hold of his neck. He wanted our kill—likely been stalking the deer himself—and we interrupted him. Might have gotten us all if it weren't for that dog. Never seen such a fierce fight, I'll give you that. Gave me time to get my knife into the beast—"

He glanced at Hunter and went silent, his jaw tight.

Mayten bent over Anatolian, turning her gaze from Adven's pain. She ran her hands over the dog's head, searching for any wounds, relieved when she found nothing but a few minor scratches among his matted fur.

"You're such a brave dog," she murmured. "Taking down that big cat."

Anatolian whined and licked her hand.

Cather finally stood and went to Adven. She reached for his shirt and he batted her hand away.

"Don't worry about me. Take care of my brother!"

"I've done what I can," Cather said in a voice so low Mayten could barely hear, "but I'm afraid Hunter's wounds are beyond my reach. He's lost too much blood and his neck is broken. He's not in pain; he cannot feel anything below his neck."

Silence filled the clearing, an unnatural quiet that made the hair on Mayten's arms stand up.

Cather must be wrong, she decided. She stared at Hunter, willing him to get up. To move.

To prove Cather wrong.

He couldn't be . . . Not kind, gentle Hunter, teller of stories with a smile that could light anyone's day . . .

A howl broke the silence and, for a moment, Mayten thought the cat had somehow come alive. Then she saw Adven's stiff back. Their leader stood at the edge of the clearing, staring at something she couldn't see.

The sound had come from him.

Cather started toward him, but Tray moved forward, grabbing her hand and pulling her to a stop.

"How long has he got?" Tray asked. His eyes pleaded, as if hoping for a different answer, but his jaw was set in a firm line.

Cather shrugged. "It's hard to tell. He comes in and out of consciousness. With the loss of blood . . . and his neck—" She swallowed, the sound loud in the almost obscene quiet. "He'd never walk again even if he could survive the blood loss. I saw this same kind of injury when we were visiting the Ocean Clan. One of the ship masons fell from a mast and landed on his head, snapping his neck. He lived two weeks and we did all we could, but he died."

Tray closed his eyes and nodded. He looked like a mirror image of his uncle, his entire body clenched in grief.

This was it, Mayten realized. The scenario Tray had explained what seemed a lifetime ago had come to pass. One of them would have to stay with Hunter and "ease his passing."

Did Cather know?

Mayten studied her friend's face, searching for words to explain what she knew had to happen. Cather gave her a sad smile, then took her arm, guiding her over to Hunter.

"Help me get some water into him."

Mayten watched in shocked silence as Cather gently removed her sweater, folded it, and pushed the bundle under the woodsman's head. She pulled a cloth from her backpack and took it to the nearby stream to wet it. Returning to Hunter's side, she gently moistened his lips with the cloth. His pale, waxy skin glistened with damp.

She couldn't tell Cather that the beautiful woodsman—this sweet, happy man—would not be cared for the way Cather would have cared for him back home.

He would die in the woods at the hands of his friends.

Mayten tried to envision the rest of the trip without him. No more stories to pass the time. No more pranking or jokes.

Her eyes burned and her breath caught. She swallowed a sob and helped Cather without knowing what she did.

ॐ

They sat with Hunter for hours. Cather cleaned the blood from Hunter's face and body, enlisting Tray's aid to change the woodsman's torn shirt.

Mayten's heart fluttered with hope the first time Hunter opened his eyes. He gave them a weak smile, then drifted off again.

Other than that, he never moved.

After a time, Cather raised his pant leg and poked his calf with a stick. He didn't flinch.

She left Mayten kneeling beside Hunter and went to inspect Anatolian. The big dog raised his head as she poked and prodded him all over, but he didn't mind. He seemed to know something was wrong. He glanced at Mayten, furry eyebrows bunched in that look that told her he was worried. She gave him a gentle smile and he laid his head back down, returning his gaze to Hunter.

Quickly, Cather wrapped a bandage around the dog's leg, then stalked over to Adven.

"Please let me tend your wounds. It's what I'm here for."

Her unspoken words seemed to hang in the air, 'I can't help your friend but I can help you.'

Adven stared at her blankly for a moment, then yanked his shirt over his head, knocking his hat off in the process.

It was the first time Mayten had seen his entire face. A long scar rippled across his left cheek at an angle up to his hairline. The puckered scar closed an empty socket where his eye had been.

Mayten involuntarily shuddered. He caught her look, glaring at her with his good eye as if daring her to comment. She held his gaze, refusing to look away, until Cather poked at something and he winced.

"Hold still," Cather said, her voice brooking no argument.

Mayten glanced at the man's chest. It was covered with blood that appeared to come from a long slash across his ribs.

"You should have let me tend this sooner," Cather said, pointing at her pack and waving Mayten over. "Now I'll need to re-open it. This has to be cleaned and sewn closed so you won't develop an infection. If treated promptly, the wound will heal. In time."

Mayten handed Cather her pack and watched in astonishment. Cather seemed another person. She'd always been a quiet girl, not speaking up unless she absolutely had to. Mayten couldn't imagine talking to Adven that way or even touching the man.

"Sit down," Cather ordered. "And hold still."

Mayten turned as her stomach roiled. She felt like she'd been running all day, exhaustion seeping into every muscle of her body.

That cat could have killed all of them—Tray, Adven, Anatolian. Tears dripped down her cheeks as she went to find solace in the one place she knew she could—the trees.

CHAPTER FIFTEEN

Mayten wanted nothing more than to surround herself with the hush of the old-growth redwoods after the scene of slaughter at the camp. She walked back through the dappled afternoon sunlight. It didn't take long for her to retrace her steps and find herself surrounded by Old Ones. Her shaking slowed as she felt their presence.

Anatolian padded quietly by her side, their footsteps cushioned by thick layers of duff. The silent sentinels around her were so tall that she couldn't see the top branches no matter how far back she craned her head. Even the air felt ancient here, unnaturally quiet.

Her bedroom was built with the wood from these trees and she felt at home in their presence. She found what she'd been looking for—a burned-out hollow in the base of one of the old giants. She crawled in and Anatolian settled next to her, positioning himself facing out of their little cave, his head resting on his injured leg.

The floor of her partial cave felt damp and smelled of rot and wisdom, the blackened ceiling inches above her head. Oddly, she couldn't smell the old burn—it could have happened ten years ago or a hundred. The injury had caused the tree to create a hard, resin-like shell that kept bugs away and allowed it to keep growing. It also created a cozy nest.

Safe. Quiet.

A stark contrast to the chaos inside her battered mind.

Anatolian was asleep within moments, sunlight caressing the top of his head. Mayten rested a hand on the dog's warm back and laid her head back against the inside of the tree as if it were her grandmother's breast. She dried her tears and tried to push the sound of the screaming cat, the smell of blood, and the pale face of her beloved woodsman from her mind.

Mayten breathed deeply of the damp, earthy smell, her jangled nerves calming. She reached out to the tree. "Thank you, old friend."

:*Welcome, child*.:

She should ask questions, see what she could find out. Wasn't that why she'd come on this infernal mission?

But she ached for home. Hunter's accident had brought on a longing to see her family, longing that hurt like a physical pain.

:*I . . . hurt*,: was all she could say. Only she hadn't said it in words, she'd *sent* the emotions . . .

:*Rest*,: the tree whispered. A flood of peaceful images washed away her anxious thoughts. She drifted off to sleep like a yet-born baby, safe in its mother's womb, comforted by the whisper of the wind in the trees, the chirp of birdsong, the sound of bees humming.

Hunger shook her awake as the smell of cooking meat made its way into her cave. Her stomach rumbled, yet she didn't want to leave her quiet sanctuary. Then she heard her name. Cather was calling her. She had to go back.

"Thank you," she breathed as she slowly crawled free of the trunk. She touched the hardened red bark of the tree and *sent* all the love she could, getting so much in return her heart felt full to bursting.

She was receiving more than emotions, she realized with a start. She could *see* images.

Level Four.

Anatolian stretched beside her as she looked up at the trees one last time, heart filled with gratitude, then headed back to camp.

"I'm coming," she yelled, hoping no one would set out to search for her.

She got back to the clearing to find the big cat's carcass had been taken away along with the bloody needles and duff. A fire burned near Hunter and huge chunks of fresh deer meat were roasting over it, filling the air with mouth-watering aromas.

Adven and Tray were in deep discussion off to one side of the fire, far enough Mayten couldn't hear their conversation. Cather kneeled next to Hunter, squeezing water onto Hunter's lips. She looked pale and exhausted.

Guilt washed over Mayten. She'd abandoned her friend— abandoned them all—just because she had to get away. She quickly crossed the clearing and kneeled next to Cather, lifting an eyebrow in question.

Cather gave a weak smile and shook her head, pressing the water-soaked cloth into Mayten's hand. Without a word, Cather rose and went to sit, back against a tree, and closed her eyes.

Hunter seemed to be resting comfortably. Mayten leaned in and kissed his cheek, wishing she could transfer some of the peace she'd received from the trees to him.

His eyes opened and he gave her a smile that was barely a shadow of his usual, bright grin. "You're very like your sisters, you know."

She rocked back on her heels. "Hunter! You can talk?"

"Of course. I'm a storyteller, it's what I do." His grin faded and she could almost see his energy draining. "I had a crush on your sister, you know."

"Taiwania?" Mayten knew she shouldn't be surprised. Most men had a crush on her beautiful sister.

"No," he said, and rolled his eyes in a way that made her laugh. "Zigba. I was the one in the story I told you. The one who tricked them."

Mayten's heart swelled and she blinked back tears, smiling at the thought of Hunter kissing Acerola who was pretending to be Zigba. "Did you ever tell her?"

He jerked as if trying to shake his head, wincing, as if the slight movement pained him. "Too shy."

She frowned. He hadn't seemed shy to her. Yet she'd been on his turf, his quest, and he wasn't in love with her. But . . . her favorite sister, the one who knitted the socks she wore on her feet—Zigba. Zigba could have married Hunter. Then he would have been her brother-in-law.

A tear slipped down her face and dripped off her chin onto the woodsman's cheek. She brushed it away with her thumb.

"I would have liked you for a brother," she said, looking into his faded green eyes. His pale face looked sheet white and the red freckles stood out like flower petals floating on water.

"Ah," he sighed, "better this way."

He was right. If Hunter had been her brother-in-law, she'd be heading home to tell Zigba of her husband's death. He knew it. She knew it.

They sat together in quiet as Tray bustled around the fire, working on dinner.

No one talked as they worked. Cather tried once to spoon broth into Hunter's mouth but he choked and coughed, then turned his head away.

Adven stomped around the camp—did he think his anger was going to change things?— suddenly stopped, looming over

Mayten. "Don't ever leave the group without telling us where you're going. Do you hear?"

Fear stopped Mayten's breath. He looked ready to shake her.

She wanted to defend herself. She'd been safe in the trees, she knew the forest, but instead she nodded, hoping he'd go away.

"You could be killed in a heartbeat," he growled before turning and stomping off.

While she'd been gone, it seemed someone had decided that Tray would move on with Cather and Mayten in the morning. Adven would stay with Hunter.

The thought made her shudder but she would be glad to be away from Adven's constant scowl.

She worked up her courage to ask a question that had been on her mind since Hunter's accident. "Adven, we've not said any thanks-giving on this quest. I'd like to do so tonight if you don't mind."

The man looked like he might spit a curse at her but he glanced at Hunter and seemed to consider.

"Do what you will," he growled and stood, disappearing into the trees.

Mayten pulled off her boots and socks, relishing the feel of cool soil beneath her feet. She kneeled on one side of Hunter, taking his hand. His arm felt odd, heavy. She couldn't lift his arm as her family did when they were in a circle so she simply held his hand. She thought about taking off his shoes too, then realized he couldn't feel the earth.

Cather pulled off her boots and took Mayten's other hand. Tray joined in, taking Hunter's other hand and completing the circle. Mayten had never led thanks-giving—that always fell to the eldest in the family. At home, that meant her da. In this circle, it meant Hunter. He looked at her and nodded, encouraging her to begin.

The cold dirt sent a chill through her body. She lifted her arms and her friends did the same, supporting Hunter as they stretched toward the stars.

Stars she couldn't see through the canopy of trees.

"Our feet are planted in the earth from which we came," Mayten said. "Our hands reach to the stars, which give us hope."

She felt her throat tighten but pressed on. "We thank you for all that we have. We trust you for all we have lost."

Her voice cracked and tears slipped down her cheeks. She saw her tears mirrored on the faces of her friends.

She took a shaky breath and continued. "For everything and everyone between the stars and the earth we give thanks to you, Great Singer."

"We give thanks to you, Great Healer," echoed Cather.

"We give thanks to you, Great Traveler," said Tray.

"Great Hunter." Hunter's voice was barely a whisper. A tear slid down his cheek, salting the earth.

CHAPTER SIXTEEN

Mayten tossed and turned, unable to get the events of
the day out of her mind. Somewhere on the far side of
the fire, she could hear Adven's voice, low and gravelly, talking
to Tray. Tears burned her eyes when she found herself looking
at Hunter's still form, Cather curled up beside him. She likely
wanted to be close by in case the woodsman needed anything.

Trying not to sob, Mayten turned away from the campfire,
laying a hand on Anatolian's warm back.

Night seemed to last forever, but finally dawn's gray light
began filtering through the trees. Mayten rolled over, her first
thought of Hunter.

He hadn't moved. Neither had Cather.

Adven rose and shook Tray's shoulder. Mayten struggled
from her blankets as Tray gently shook Cather's shoulder. Evidently, the healer had managed some sleep.

Anatolian huffed, standing and stretching before heading
into the trees. Adven threw a log on the fire which sparked
to life. The tang of campfire smoke burned Mayten's nostrils.
She rubbed at her gritty eyes, then quickly filled her pack and
shouldered it. Tray handed her a chunk of cooked meat with
an apologetic grimace. Anatolian came back in time to whuff at

Tray and got his own hunk of meat as a reward. Tray patted the big dog's head.

"No time to heat coffee this morning. Adven wants us headed out."

Mayten nodded, unwilling to trust her voice. Somewhere above, a bird sang its morning song, the song jangling like broken bells against her heavy heart. She moved to Hunter's side, her feet as leaden as her soul.

Tray and Cather had evidently said their goodbyes while she was packing. Tray stood next to Cather, awkwardly patting her shoulder. Tears shone on Cather's cheeks, but she shrugged her pack on and waited as Mayten bent down to kiss Hunter's cheek.

His eyes fluttered open and he spoke softly, his voice weaker than the day before. She had to bend close to hear his words. "He's . . . not . . . a . . . bad . . . man."

Mayten glanced at Adven standing, arms crossed, next to Tray and Cather, a deeper scowl than usual on his face.

"Try to . . . see the . . . good in him." The effort seemed to drain the last of the woodsman's strength. His eyes slipped closed.

"Time to go. Day is wasting," Adven said.

Mayten scowled back at him. She leaned so low her lips almost brushed Hunter's ear. "I'll try for you, Hunter. For you. And I'll always remember you as my brother."

She brushed her lips across his cheek, stood, and stalked past Adven, giving a savage grin when her pack knocked his shoulder as she passed.

☙

For a long time the trio walked in silence, staying closer to each other than they normally did. Mayten didn't know about the others, but she needed to be close to her friends.

They were leaving gentle Hunter to die in the forest.

She would never see him again.

The forest somehow felt less friendly than it had before. Mayten found herself flinching at the snap of a twig. The stories of bears and boars now seemed a threatening reality instead of a funny tale.

She'd been an idiot to wander through the forest alone yesterday. Adven had been right to be angry with her.

I've got to get my mind off what happened.

Mayten drew a deep breath and focused on the trees instead of Hunter. All around her, aspens whispered in the early morning breeze, new leaves shining like bright green coins as they caught the sun.

She cleared her mind, opened her soul to whatever the trees wanted to show her as she walked. Nothing happened at first. She remembered the messages she'd received from the redwoods, the feel of being *inside* the grandmother tree.

Just as Mayten was ready to give up, convinced she'd been dreaming, the visions flowed in.

The aspens sent pictures of their history. They were all connected, Mayten realized. As though they'd all come from the same root source yet were not the same. They were introducing themselves to her in a new way, building a deeper relationship. She could almost see distinct personalities as she brushed the awareness of different trees. Was one shy, another almost demanding her attention?

Her vision of the trees kept expanding, getting bigger. The trees were so much more than she'd originally thought. They were individuals, but they were also connected by species like the people in her clan. Broader still, they connected through their root system to each other and through birds and insects who traveled among them like messengers, connecting throughout the island. She suspected they were connected beyond the island somehow, but the thought overwhelmed her.

Ø

They walked through the day taking only one short break and eventually found a nice flat spot to stop for the night. The trees opened up into a small meadow. Each camp felt the same, yet each was lovely in its own way. Mayten and Cather started toward the far side of the camp to gather wood.

Tray turned and then paused. "Guess I'll go over there and gather some wood." He pointed in the opposite direction of the girls.

That was their normal routine—she and Cather would go one way and he'd go the other. Was he too torn in his new role as leader to admit that he was scared?

"Wait," Cather said, "Could you maybe stay with us? You know, for protection?"

"Sure," he agreed, relief evident on his face. "For protection."

They moved through the trees together, gathering small branches and broken twigs for the fire.

Once again, Cather proved she understood boys in a way Mayten never could. But false dependence? Was that what boys wanted in a girl?

If it was, she'd be lucky to ever find a mate. She'd never know when to pretend to need help.

There had to be men like her da, Mayten decided as she added another branch to the pile in her arms. He was good and kind and didn't seem to mind her mother's strength and confidence. One time she had entered the kitchen and heard him say to her mother, "Castanea, you're as stubborn as a mule, but I wouldn't have it any other way."

Then they'd kissed. It seemed like her parents were always kissing, which was why she had so many brothers and sisters.

Still, if there were men like her da in the world, maybe someday she'd find one worth kissing.

Once again, she found herself missing her family—even her mother—so much it hurt. Her anger toward her mother was a thing of the past. What if she died out here like Hunter? What if the last thing her mother had to remember her by was a grumpy scowl?

She'd almost filled her arms when she noticed Cather and Tray working side by side. Cather bent down to pick up another branch and placed it on the wood already piled high in Tray's arms. Tray just watched, a silly grin stretching his face wide.

Could it be that Cather's years of waiting for that hard-headed boy-child were finally paying off? Just because Cather pretended to need his protection?

Or was it the close brushes with death they'd experienced over the last two days?

Maybe, she thought a bit more generously, his being thrust into a leadership position, to bear the responsibility of being a man, had made him more aware that Cather was a woman.

Mayten snorted and headed back to the camp with her armload of wood, whistling for Anatolian to follow. Anatolian had been rolling in the dirt and was a dusty mess. She dumped her load of wood and found a small pinecone.

"Come on, boy. Let's get you cleaned up."

Anatolian's tongue lolled from his mouth as she worked carefully to untangle his knots and get rid of the burs and dust. She had the fire started and Hunter's pot simmering with a meat stew by the time the other two wandered in.

"Took you long enough," she said, surprised at the pang that made her stomach feel pinched. She was happy for them— but why did they have to stay gone so long?

The glowing smile on Cather's face made the world seem brighter. Mayten's foul mood melted. She couldn't be mad at her friends. It would be nice if at least one good thing came out of this trip.

She had a chance to reconsider her position during dinner. She'd never seen so many 'googly eyes' before.

Finally, she could stomach it no longer. "Tray, what did Adven tell you about the cat's attack? Why didn't Hunter sense the cat? Don't woodsmen learn to sense animals—especially dangerous ones—as part of their calling?"

Tray picked up a handful of pine needles and tossed them into the fire one by one. The needles flashed into flame, quickly curling into ash. The smell of burning pine sap hung in the air.

"Adven and Hunter were arguing about something," he finally said. "That's why Hunter didn't sense the lion. Adven was pretty broken up about it. Thought it was his fault."

Mayten snorted. "Broken up? That's hard to picture."

Tray jumped to his feet. "How can you say that? Hunter was like a little brother to Adven. And what he has to do . . . you have no idea how hard that will be."

Mayten flushed with guilt. She'd never seen Tray this angry before. "I'm sorry, Tray. I shouldn't have said that. I've just never seen him anything *but* mad. I don't know why he hates me."

"It's not just you. He hates all singers."

Mayten flushed with heat that had nothing to do with the fire. Singers were gentle people, loved by everybody. She bolted to her feet, facing him across the fire. "What has a singer ever done to hurt him?"

Tray glared at her. He opened his mouth. Shut it again.

Anatolian rose and pressed against her leg, alert, but looking a bit confused.

Cather stood and placed her hand on Tray's shoulder.

"I would like to know," Mayten said more softly.

"That story isn't mine to tell, but I can tell you this—Adven and Hunter were arguing about you." Tray jabbed his finger at her. "That's why Hunter didn't sense the mountain lion."

"About me?" Mayten felt as though he'd punched her in the stomach. Her breath whooshed out, taking her anger with it. She sank slowly back down to the ground, knees crumpling beneath her.

Was *she* to blame for Hunter's death?

"Why were they arguing about me?" Had she done something wrong? If so, what? She held her breath, afraid of the answer.

"Adven didn't think you should have come on this quest and Hunter thought you should. He stood up for you and it made Adven mad." Tray glanced away, kicking at the dirt with his toe.

Mayten didn't want to fight. She wanted to crawl back in her tree and shut the world out. She'd known Adven didn't like her, she just hadn't known why.

"It wasn't my idea. I never wanted to come."

Cather cut in, her hands around Tray's upper arm. "Look, we're all upset about Hunter but we need to stay strong. We're a team. And what do you mean about how hard it will be, Tray? What does Adven have to do?"

Tray and Mayten stared at each other across the fire. Finally, Tray sat back down, picked up another handful of pine needles, and tossed them one by one into the fire. Cather sat next to him, clearly waiting for an answer.

It was just as clear to Mayten that Tray was done talking. She looked into Cather's gentle eyes.

"The questers have a rule—" she started.

"A code," Tray broke in.

"A code," she repeated with a sigh. "If one of their own gets hurt and they are too far from home or help and are so bad they can't be helped—"

"And there's no other option," Tray added defensively.

"After two days, they have to . . ." she stopped, unable to go on.

"They have to ease the injured person's passing." Tray scrubbed his hands on his knees.

Mayten was sure Cather would explode. Healers fought to save lives, not take them. But Cather sat in silence, brushing a tear from her cheek.

"Healers have a similar . . . understanding, although we don't call it a code. When someone is dying, when death is inevitable and they are in pain." Mayten could barely hear her friend's soft voice. "We have herbs to ease their way."

Mayten didn't know what to say. Was she the only one who hadn't known that some of her people were helping others die?

Not only did she *feel* naive, she was embarrassed to *be* so naive. Was that why Adven hated singers. Did he think singers were gutless people, vomiting when they should be helping and falling asleep in trees at important times. Did he consider singers to be wasters-of-air that had to be protected from the harsher realities of life?

It looked like singers weren't as loved by everyone as she'd thought. Perhaps singers—her entire family—were only tolerated.

For the first time in her life Mayten wondered if she really knew anything about the world.

She pulled out her blanket and lay down, calling Anatolian to her. Cather stayed by Tray's side. Mayten turned away from them, struggling not to feel rejected by her friends. She listened to the murmur of their voices late into the night, burying her face in Anatolian's fur to hide her tears.

She'd never felt so unwanted, unneeded, and unnecessary. Why had she even come?

The king asked for me.

But how was she supposed to help if she never really got a chance to listen to the trees?

Mayten rubbed the star-shaped rock in her pocket, overcome by the fierce need to be home.

The one place she knew she belonged.

CHAPTER SEVENTEEN

The next two days passed in a blur. Mayten sank deeper into a dark mood while Cather and Tray told each other story after story. They'd spent the last fifteen years together—where did they find so many new stories?

Not only was there a nauseating overabundance of googly eyes, the pair constantly teased each other. And the giggles . . . all those giggles.

You'd think they were meeting each other for the first time.

"Come on, Mayten, walk with us!" Cather called when the trail widened and the trees opened up, letting in more sunlight.

They could walk side by side, Mayten knew that, but she hesitated. "Thanks, but I'd rather be alone."

It wasn't Cather and Tray, not entirely. Mayten felt as though something was sucking her soul dry. Color seemed to drain from her world, turning everything gray.

Cather's smile faded as she turned away, walking quietly by Tray's side.

Every now and then, Tray would drop back and attempt to tease a smile out of Mayten. She tried to give him that smile, to let him think all was well, but she could not shake off the heaviness weighing her down.

She turned in early every night. Anatolian seemed to sense her distress, staying pressed against her side except when he hunted. She fell asleep clinging to her star rock, one hand on Anatolian's back.

On the third day, Mayten struggled awake, wrapped in the dark haze she couldn't seem to shake. Trees and sky and ground blurred together, without color, without light. She forced one foot in front of the other, feeling more like a puppet than a person, not noticing the others had stopped until she almost ran into Cather.

Cather pointed at a long, fallen log and they all sat, sharing water as they rested. The water was refreshing and the act of drinking brought Mayten back into her body, starting to clear her foggy brain.

Tray was being his goofy self, trying to make Cather laugh. Mayten was lost in her own thoughts when Cather said, "Look Tray, that frog is red. I've never seen such a thing. Isn't it beautiful?"

"You want a frog? A frog shall be yours," Tray said in a gallant tone. He leaped from the trunk with a deep bow. A sense of urgency slithered through Mayten's sluggish brain. She jumped off the log and grabbed Tray's arm as he reached for the frog.

Snap! The frog vanished.

Tray stepped back, almost tromping on Mayten's foot. He wiggled his fingers and jerked his chin at the large lizard who blended right into the bark of the tree. "Did you see that?"

Cather moved to Tray's side, taking his hand and studying it.

"I moved in time," Tray said. "If Mayten hadn't . . ." He gave her a curious look. "Did you actually see the lizard? Or—"

"I didn't," Mayten said abruptly. "It's just that you almost grabbed a poisonous frog. The pretty ones often are. Though, that one evidently wasn't poisonous . . . or maybe that lizard has developed an immunity."

They decided their break was over and Tray led them up the trail. Mayten lost track of time as she trudged along. A fine mist rolled in, soaking her hair and clothing. The dampness added to the darkness enveloping her.

She was sick of walking, sick of the clouds and not being able to see the sky, sick of venison.

Sick of the endless questions that swirled in her brain: Why did Adven hate singers? Had she really caused Hunter's death? Would he still be alive if she'd stayed home?

Gradually, she became aware of other images interweaving with her own, images of trees dying—not just a few trees, acres of trees. A sense of pain, death, and despair washed through her. Each step became a battle to keep moving, her mind blanketed in fog and mist.

There was something she was supposed to be doing, but she couldn't remember what.

Mayten had no idea how much time passed before Tray stopped again, this time for lunch. The images in her mind, the sense of death and despair, the *knowing* she should be doing something—

She was losing her mind, she decided. She slid to the ground, using a pine—as big around as two men standing back to back—for a backrest, and closed her eyes. Anatolian nosed her hand, then headed into the bushes to find his own lunch.

:*Help us!*:

Startled, Mayten scanned their group but Cather and Tray looked fine chatting and flirting. Was someone lost close by? Someone who needed help?

The image of Hunter lying so still on the ground, buried in blankets, slid into her mind. But the voice she'd heard hadn't been Adven or Hunter's . . .

Tray and Cather were sitting on a rock sharing their food. They hadn't seen Adven for three days now. So who . . . ?

Mayten grabbed her head, feeling like she'd been struck in the head by another pinecone. Trees and ground spun around her as she realized what she'd been feeling wasn't about Adven or Hunter. The sadness and despair she'd been experiencing were not *her* emotions at all.

It came from the trees.

Their combined pain was so intense she drew it from the ground itself.

"I need some time to listen to the trees," Mayten said, not really caring if anyone heard. "They are really distressed. I need to pay attention, to listen."

Tray handed Cather another piece of venison and nodded. "We should reach the castle before dinner so we have time."

Mayten bit back a frown. Her spending time with the trees gave *him* more time alone with Cather.

She scrambled to her feet and wandered through the pines and firs, trying to decide where to put her attention. Wild oaks were sprinkled in with the pine—scarlet oaks, white oaks, and bur oaks were easily recognized.

Then she spotted the perfect place—the base of a live oak.

Huge branches spread their arms wide from the ancient tree, reminding her of her favorite auntie back home. She approached slowly, feeling like she was greeting an old friend. Her fingers brushed the rough trunk, gently savoring the musty smell. She jumped up and grabbed the lowest branch, pulling herself higher into the welcoming branches.

It had been ten days since she'd climbed a tree and she reveled in the feel of bark beneath her hands, the stretch and pull of her muscles. Anatolian whuffed as she climbed, evidently finished with his lunch. He curled up at the base of the tree, keeping his head up, as if on guard duty.

She found a comfortable spot to sit on a branch so thick it could have been a bench. She settled back against the trunk and began to relax. Her breathing slowed and her mind cleared. She listened to the buzz of insects, the cry of crows. The darkness that she'd been living with lifted as she breathed in and out, in and out.

Why didn't you seek the trees earlier? a voice whispered in her mind. *You'll never be a proper tree singer unless you listen to the trees.*

I'm listening to them now, she told the voice. *So hush.*

She listened for the tree's life story first. Each tree had a story of its own, connected to the others through collective consciousness yet individual to itself. This tree, almost three hundred years old, had a male essence and had seen and heard many things over the years.

:*Little sister.*: The oak's 'voice' soothed her mind, driving the lingering fog away.

Mayten let a soft breath slide from her lips. :*Uncle, what is unsettling your peace?*:

Pictures tumbled through her mind, images as disturbing as they were confusing. The face of a man from a time long ago, perhaps two hundred years according to the oak. The man had pale skin, black, curly hair, and a thin black mustache. Tall and thin, the man had a haughty look about his eyes.

Why was the oak showing her this man? What did he have to do with what was happening?

Another wave of images crowded out the first. An image that indicated an imbalance in the seasons, and something that seemed like an emptiness . . . or perhaps death . . . of living things.

She tried to grab hold of the images, make some sense of what she was seeing, but had no idea how one related to the other.

What could a man who lived hundreds of years ago have to do with the trees and plants living now?

What was the emptiness, a feeling so dark it made her shiver with fear?

The imbalance of seasons . . . the emptiness . . . It felt as though nature had been knocked off its feet and couldn't fight back.

She clutched at the branch, fearing she might be sick. What was the tree trying to tell her? :*I don't understand, Uncle. Help me understand.*:

She listened closely, keeping her mind clear. But Uncle seemed to have said what he had to say.

A new feeling bubbled to life. A feeling she couldn't identify. She found herself thinking about a walk she had taken with her mother when she was a few years younger than Wollemi. They were far from their homestead in a barren part of the forest where the ancient pinion pines grew. Mayten had just settled on a rock when she heard a rattling noise. She'd been jerked off the rock and shoved behind her mother. She watched her mother use her walking stick to beat a snake over and over and over.

After the snake was dead, Mother told her to always check for snakes before sitting. One bite from a snake like that one would kill a full-grown adult.

Mother's voice shook as she explained. Even then, Mayten knew her mother had an overwhelming fear of snakes. She never went near a snake if it wandered close to the homestead, instead calling Da to carry the snake away.

Mayten remembered being terrified at first—of her mother. Mother had turned into a stranger acting to protect her child, not a woman who hated and feared snakes.

Something had strengthened her mother, made her brave enough to protect her child.

The violent death made Mayten feel scared—and protected.

The memories shifted, replaced by other images—of home. Taiwania singing, the twins laughing, Oleaster working, Wollemi holding up a kitten for her to see, her parent's faces, eyes filled with love. The visions were so real she reached out her hand, wanting to pet the kitten—

She snatched back her hand, cradling it to her chest as though bit. Wollemi didn't have a kitten. Their family had never had a kitten. Why was she seeing Wollemi with a kitten?

And the twins—their bellies looked even more swollen than when she'd left.

Was it possible her mother was sending pictures through the trees?

The thought created a jumble of questions—were these images of what was happening *now*? How long did it take a message to travel through the trees? Why was Mother sending the images? *Was* Mother sending them?

As though someone had dumped cold water on her head, the questions fled Mayten's mind, leaving her clear-headed for the first time in days.

Of course, Mother had sent the images. Somehow she knew Mayten would need her family. She wanted Mayten to know her family loved her, that they were thinking of her.

Warmth flooded through her, filling the emptiness, driving out the pain. Tears rolled down her cheeks and dripped from her chin. Mayten brushed the tears away, remembering her family, each wonderful face.

Peace settled over her, bringing with it a sense of calm. Joy lit the darkness she'd lived with since Hunter's accident . . . and before.

She sat up straight, feeling the oak's rough support against her back. She had to send a message back. To let Mother know about Hunter so she could send word to his parents in the Ocean Clan.

But how?

Mayten let the sadness and pain return as she focused on an image of their little group saying thanks-giving over Hunter's still form. After a few moments spent concentrating on that image, she brought up an image of the three of them safely sitting on a log, then changed the image to one of Anatolian resting below her. Reluctantly, she focused on an image of Adven and his scowl. The clan needed to know he was alive, but she didn't have to like sending it.

Exhausted, Mayten let the images slip from her mind. Her knees trembled, along with her hands and arms.

Would her sending work? Would Mother receive the images?

Guilt flashed through her as she realized she'd forgotten the most important message of all. Quickly, she cleared her mind, ignoring her exhaustion, and focused on the images received from the oak—the face of the man shown to her and the imbalance and emptiness.

That was the hardest of all. How did one picture emptiness? She finally settled on an image of dying trees.

Was this why she'd never heard of anyone communicating in this manner? Because it was so hard to put an image to feelings?

Would her mother be able to understand her message? Would she know what Mayten was trying to say?

On instinct, she focused on the memory of her mother saving her from the snake. The awe she felt at that memory, safe, loved, protected. That memory had helped her understand.

Would it also convey to Mother how sorry Mayten was? Would her mother recognize it as her way of saying, "I'm sorry?"

Holding the memory in her mind, focused on the *sending*, Mayten felt a fierce, protective instinct fill her with strength and clarity.

She didn't know when, she didn't know how, but she would find out what or who was hurting her trees and she would stop it. That was a promise: to the trees, to herself, and to her mother.

CHAPTER EIGHTEEN

Mayten scrambled from the tree and hurried back to the others, Anatolian at her heels.

Cather straightened, putting one hand on the rock, and stared at her, cheeks red. "Did you learn anything?"

Tray jumped to his feet and helped Cather stand as they both looked expectantly at her.

"Listen," Mayten said. "I don't really understand what I saw. There is something terrible happening to the trees. I can't make any sense out of it yet, but we need to get going right now."

"Okay, then." Tray pulled on his pack, then helped Cather with hers. Mayten swung her pack from the ground and slid it on, shrugging her shoulders to settle the load as they headed down the trail.

Cather slowed her steps until Mayten caught up. They walked in silence for a few moments, thoughts tumbling about Mayten's mind like a feather caught in river rapids.

"Did it work?" Cather finally asked. "What did you hear?"

For the first time in days, Mayten was ready to talk. She kept her eyes on the trail. "It was more like a series of pictures in my mind. Something is taking the trees' life or energy or . . . I don't know how to say it exactly. And there's this man, but he lived two hundred years ago, so I can't think out how he figures into this, but I could feel great resentment from the trees toward him. I need more information."

She glanced at Cather . . . who was—of course—watching Tray.

"You're really happy, aren't you?" she asked Cather.

Her friend smiled and shrugged. "I am. I'm sorry, I know this is important, I just . . ."

"I'm happy for you." Mayten squeezed Cather's arm. "What's happening to you is important too."

Cather blushed. "It is, isn't it? I was afraid it would never happen. I'm so glad you understand. I feel like I've been ignoring you and you've been so down."

"I know you've wanted Tray's attention forever. What do you think changed? Why now?"

"I'm not sure. We have two years until we can declare ourselves at the gathering, but it seems like he's—"

A shout from Tray caught their attention. "Come quick! You've got to see this!"

They raced up the trail, Anatolian in the lead. Legs burning, Mayten stopped on Tray's right while Cather moved to his left. The last part of the trail had been steep enough she was soon gasping for breath and could hear Cather doing the same.

"Have you ever seen anything like it?" Tray asked, his voice filled with awe.

The trees ended abruptly, opening on a vista so bright Mayten's eyes hurt. Below them a lush green valley bordered an impossibly blue sea. She blinked and squinted, letting her eyes adjust to the brilliance so different from the dark forest. Anatolian yipped like a puppy, tail wagging so hard his entire body shook.

"Look!" Cather pointed at a wooded area partway through the valley. "There's the castle."

Three stone-gray turrets jutted high above the oak trees. Flags flying the king's lion crest waved as if in welcome. A gentle breeze brushed a strand of hair off her cheek, bringing strange scents along with it. She'd only visited the Ocean Clan once and memories of the smells of brine and fish flooded through her.

"We did it." Mayten grabbed Tray and hugged him tight, Cather joining in. The relief of finally seeing their destination felt like waking up having forgotten it was your birthday and being greeted with hugs and well wishes from the family.

"Let's go," said Tray, echoing Mayten's desire to get to the castle. They raced down the hillside, laughing with relief. Mayten's heart felt free after so long in despair. She had a new sense of urgency that lifted the darkness from her soul. The soft, moist air seemed to wash her whole being clean.

Then a thought made her stop. "Wait," she yelled.

Tray slid to a stop on the rocky hillside and Cather knocked into him. He caught her when she started to slip.

"What is it?" he yelled.

Mayten stumbled down to them. "Look at us. We can't meet the king looking like this."

They hadn't bathed since they left home. Tray's neck looked nearly black and Cather, though Mayten knew she had tried to keep her hands clean, had dirt under her fingernails. Her own hair was a tangled mess and her clothes were stiff with sweat and dirt.

"You're right," Cather said. "We need to find a place to wash and change before we meet the king."

Tray squinted at the valley below, shading his eyes from the sun with an arm. "I see a lake." He pointed at a small lake along the trail to the castle.

"Perfect," she said. "Let's go."

Again, they ran laughing down the slope. Dirt clouds flew around them as they ran, causing more dust to stick to Mayten's sweaty skin. The hill flattened out at the bottom and ended in a path of stone. They crossed the path, hurrying over some kind of short grasses she had never seen. The rich-smelling grasses made her nose itch.

As they got closer to the lake, Mayten realized they were entering the castle grounds. The trees were pink with cherry blossoms, something Mayten had only heard about. The pink color against the green grass was more than beautiful. The hedges were groomed to look like animals: lions, bears, and some fanciful creatures like dragons lined the perfectly cut grasses. They slowed as they approached the lake—which was really more of a large pond.

Tray put his fists on his hips and frowned. "Do you think it will be okay to bathe here?"

Mayten glanced around. There was no one in sight and the castle was hidden by a row of tall, thin trees she had no name for. They were planted close together as if to block the castle from view. "I think we'll be okay. It's better than walking into the castle like this."

She patted her tunic, sending a cloud of dust into the air, coughing as she waved the dust away with one hand.

"See those rocks?" She pointed at a large stack of rocks that jutted into the water, creating a natural divider. "We'll go in on the right, and you take the left, Tray. We'll wash as fast as we can."

"Sounds good." Tray sprinted toward the water, taking off his shirt as he ran. Anatolian rushed past him and splashed into the water first. Mayten laughed.

"He's got the right idea," Cather said. "I didn't feel dirty until now and suddenly I can't wait to get into that water!"

Mayten ran down the lake's edge, Cather close behind. Quickly, they stripped off their clothes. Mayten fished a lump of soap from her pack, grateful that her sister had insisted she take it.

Cather took out her rain poncho and unrolled it, pulling out a small ceramic jar and holding it up for Mayten to see. "It didn't break!"

She pried off the lid. The smell of lilacs filled the air. "It's soap to wash our hair."

The ice-cold water took her breath away, but never had Mayten enjoyed a bath more. She'd never been this dirty before, either. She scrubbed her arms, blushing as the dirt washed away in murky clouds, leaving behind clean skin of a completely different color. How she must stink!

At least the others were just as dirty. Funny what you could get used to.

She wished she had time to wash her clothes as well, but that wasn't going to happen. She'd just have to wear the least dirty ones. Thankfully, they'd kept their ceremonial aprons packed away. The aprons should cover the worst of the dirt.

Despite being cold, the water felt so good she and Cather were soon laughing and splashing. She'd just rinsed the suds from Cather's hair when a deep voice interrupted her.

"What have we here?"

Mayten and Cather shrieked, dropping low in the water. A horse and rider moved out of the trees. The rider looked to be about their age, perhaps a little older. He glared down at them, brow furrowed so deeply his thick black eyebrows met in a stern line. His skin tone favored the island's original inhabitants, a golden brown. His hair, long and wavy, brushed his shoulders, and his nose—a bit too large for his face—gave him a hawkish appearance.

"Swimming in the king's pond without permission. Whatever shall I do with you?"

King's pond? Was this the groundskeeper, then? Would he arrest them? *Could* he arrest them?

The young man dressed like one of the people who worked in her brother's fields, all in brown with a dirty shirt and disheveled hair.

Water splashed on the far side of the rock pile.

"They're with me, sir." Tray's voice was pitched lower than usual and was accompanied by Anatolian's low growl.

Was he trying to sound older?

Mayten bit her lip, wondering how effective lowering his voice would be if Tray was standing naked on the other side of the rocks. He was likely shivering as much as she was.

Another growl helped boost her confidence. Anatolian was a large dog and could be intimidating.

"I'm leading the questing team the king sent for," Tray said. Try as she might, Mayten couldn't hear any shivers in his voice. "We were unwilling to come before the king in our dirty condition after ten days of traveling."

The rider moved the horse until he could—at least she thought he could—see Tray. "And you are?"

The imperious tone of his voice set her teeth on edge.

"I'm Tray Traveler, sir. The ladies are Mayten Singer and Cather Healer. Our woodsman was injured three days back and our team leader, Adven Traveler, my uncle, sent us ahead as the king's summons seemed urgent."

"The king is familiar with Adven." The rider turned back to the girls.

Mayten shivered, wishing the rider would go away. She needed to get out of the water before—

"Which one of you is the singer?"

"That would be me, sir." She didn't know why she—why *they*—were calling the rider, a boy barely older than they were, "sir." There was something in the way he carried himself, she realized. Did everyone who worked at the castle act this way?

She almost asked who he was and what he did, but stopped herself. For some reason asking such a question didn't feel appropriate.

"All right, Mayten Singer," the rider said with a brisk nod. "I will tell the king of your arrival. He will be ready to meet you at evening meal. Healer, the queen will want to see you. She's not well and our healers haven't been able to help. Until then, I suggest you dry off."

He smirked and spurred his horse, disappearing almost immediately into the trees.

She didn't like the rider. Not at all. He seemed to enjoy intimidating them.

"You girls okay?" Tray called from the other side of the rocks.

"F-f-f-ine," said Cather, shivering so hard Mayten could barely understand her. "Just c-c-c-old."

"Go ahead and get dressed," Tray said. "I'll keep an eye out for more company."

Mayten gratefully waded from the water, grabbing the blanket tied to the bottom of her pack. She shook the blanket out and wrapped it around her shoulders. Not the cleanest way to dry herself but the blanket was warm.

Cather did the same.

Anatolian trotted up and shook, spraying water everywhere. Mayten shrieked, using her blanket as a shield, then finished drying off. She yanked on the cleanest clothes she could find, then pulled her apron from the pack. The apron was thoroughly wrinkled, but it was clean. "I'm glad Adven told us to take these off."

"Me too," Cather said with a nod. She raised her voice. "We're dressed, Tray."

He came around the rock jetty, pulling on his shirt.

"Who do you think that was?" Mayten asked, grateful to have stopped shivering. Cather oiled, finger combed, and braided Mayten's hair as they sat on the grass.

Tray rolled his eyes and plopped on the grass beside them. "I don't know but I guess we'll find out soon enough."

CHAPTER NINETEEN

Mayten followed Tray from the pond up the path as he led the way toward the castle. Their plan to arrive unannounced had failed, leaving her feeling more sheepish than confident.

The entrance to the castle faced the sea, which sparkled in the sunlight. The blue of the water was deep, almost black, and a briny smell filled the warm afternoon air. Up close the castle appeared rather small, probably no bigger than two of Mayten's homes. But it did have two stories and was made of carved stones, a much grander design than any building Mayten had ever seen.

Were the stones of the castle found close by or had they been brought in by ship?

They walked around the side of the castle which was visible in glimpses through the trees. This brought them to the front and a cobblestone path led from there up to a wooden gate. The gate was firmly shut, blocking the entrance to the castle. Two guards wearing leather helms and tall boots stood sentry in front of the gate. The castle's second story stood high above the wall with several arched windows facing the sea. Mayten lost her breath as she gazed up at the fabled castle. Up close, it was a rather imposing building. The windows looked huge, taller than she was.

What would it be like to wake up to that view every day?

Though her village faced the sea, it was still at least a two-day walk to get to the Ocean Clan where her sisters lived. She'd only visited once for a festival and she'd been ten at the time. There had been more sand and less rocks on the beaches of the Ocean Clan.

The coastline here was rugged and wild. Just looking at the ocean made her stomach feel queasy. It all looked so vast, so empty.

How had her sisters adjusted to life by the ocean? She would much rather look at the trees, which felt cozy and welcoming. Mayten made a mental note to ask her sisters that very question when she got home.

If she got home.

The darkness she'd been experiencing the past few days nudged the edges of her mind, a darkness so sinister she wondered if anyone could defeat it.

The guards moved to open the gate. Evidently the men had been warned of their approach.

"There's not much security here," Tray whispered as they passed through the gate. "These two guards are well past their prime which tells me the king doesn't think there's much of a threat. He has a whole garrison of soldiers if he needs them. I wonder where they are?"

"As I understand it," Mayten said, "the threat is not to the castle, but to the trees and to the seasons."

"The seasons?" Tray raised an eyebrow.

"It's hard to explain . . ." She stopped. They were standing in an enormous yard covered with a tough grass she had never seen before. Carved wooden children's toys and buckets and large spoons cluttered the yard. A woman and a boy, wearing simple clothes of a thin material, were pulling a wagon across the lawn and piling the toys into it as fast as they could. Two men, similarly dressed, were clipping the uneven grass and trimming hedges.

"I think we got here sooner than they expected," said Tray. "They seem to be cleaning up. Maybe it's a good thing we were seen at the pond."

"Feels a bit like home," Mayten said, nodding at the toys. "Does the king have a lot of children?"

"I don't know," said Tray. "People seem to like him. But . . . I guess I never paid much attention to anything else."

"I heard he's handsome." Cather blushed and Tray's eyes narrowed. "And that he does have quite a few children."

A portly, older man with skin like old leather stood in front of the large wooden doors. The man wore a green cap and matching shirt with puffed sleeves, and his face was flushed as if he'd been rushing around. His short brown pants were tucked into front-laced, knee-high boots. He took off his hat in a sweeping bow.

"Welcome," he said, in a rather high voice. His mustache was waxed into two round curls and his beard had been combed into a sharp triangle.

Mayten clenched her teeth against the giggle bubbling in her throat. Judging by the sparkle in Cather's eyes, her friend was suffering the same trouble.

"I'm Sir Thornton Underbrush, the king's secretary."

Mayten clenched her jaw even harder.

"The king has asked me to greet you and make you comfortable before dinner. Madam Singer?" The man glanced from Mayten to Cather.

"Yes," Mayten said.

"Is this your dog?" He stared at Anatolian, still wet from his recent swim and smelling rather musky.

"Yes, sir. His name is Anatolian."

The man snapped his fingers. The young boy with curly dark hair dropped the toy he'd just picked up into the wagon and ran up to them, grinning. "Take the dog and wash it good, Edward. When the animal is dry you may take it to the singer's room."

Anatolian looked at her with worried eyes, but Mayten couldn't see a way to get around the secretary's request. She patted Anatolian's back and signaled for him to go.

"Thank you, Sir Underbrush," Tray said. Mayten wondered at his ability to say the name without laughing.

In her clan, names indicated a family's calling. What kind of calling could *Underbrush* belong to? The pulling of weeds?

"I'm Tray Traveler. This is Cather Healer."

Sir Underbrush bowed low again, his belly lapping over his belt and straining his shirt buttons. She got the feeling it had been a while since he'd worn these clothes.

Was the king trying to show off for his visitors or was Sir Underbrush? This whole welcome seemed oddly confusing. She'd expected castle life to be more organized.

They followed Sir Underbrush through the entrance into the castle and found they were standing in a high-ceilinged room. Beyond the room stretched a long, narrow hallway with arched, open doorways on either side. She could just make out a flight of stairs at the far end of the hall.

Light from the second-story windows cast long shadows down the hall. The secretary led the way, his gait more waddle than walk. His pants strained at the seams as he moved.

The poor guy must be miserable.

Sir Underbrush stopped in front of the first open archway to the right and gestured for them to enter. Mayten's mouth fell open. She had expected something elegant and kingly. Instead, they entered a large sitting room with overstuffed leather couches and chairs in a variety of patterns. A large bookcase filled one part of the room, shelves stuffed full of books that looked like they had actually been read. Books were lying open on tables and those in the bookcase lay at odd angles in no discernible arrangement.

She'd never seen so many books in one place!

A variety of overlapping rugs of various sizes and a cacophony of colors made the room feel warm, cozy, and slightly confused as if it were a room well lived in. *The king must be more interested in comfort than order.*

"I'll have the servants bring you something from the kitchen while your rooms are being prepared," Sir Underbrush said. He gave a brief bow . . . and something ripped

Mayten covered her mouth, biting a knuckle to keep from laughing.

Sir Underbrush flushed, backed out of the room . . . and bumped into a great bear of a man with a bushy red beard and a mass of black hair. The newcomer's skin reminded her of teakwood. He had a broad, flat nose and full lips, not unlike the lumbermen who helped her mother manage the forest.

The man took one look at Sir Underbrush and bellowed a laugh, slapping him on the shoulder so hard that the secretary took a step forward.

"Good heavens, Thornton," the bearded man boomed. "What on earth are you wearing?"

"You told me to greet the guests, sir. I just thought . . ."

"I told you to greet them, not scare them to death. Go and change at once, you look ridiculous." He moved to one side and gave the secretary a push out the doorway.

Sir Underbrush gave them an embarrassed look and dashed away, both hands covering his backside.

"Welcome, welcome!" sang the bearded man, a man who seemed to fill the room. Who was this giant that he would treat the king's secretary with such odd familiarity?

"I'm sorry if Thornton scared you," the man continued. "His da served my grandfather, you see, who immigrated from Sapia as a child, and was much more, shall we say—*traditional*—than I and sometimes he gets confused. I'm Thomas Redmond or King Redmond if you prefer."

He reached for her hand as he spoke. Mayten thought her hand might be crushed, but the *king* kept his grip gentle. He bowed slightly, smiling right at her, his dark eyes twinkling. There was a space between his two front teeth that Mayten found oddly appealing.

"*You're* the king?" Shocked, she blurted out the first thing that came to mind. This man's casual bearing and appearance—he couldn't be the king. Could he?

She had to admit her expectations were based on stories she'd heard as a child or in books. In those stories, kings sat on big thrones wearing crowns and richly embroidered robes and holding scepters.

This man looked like a neighbor who'd just stopped by to help with the chores. He even smelled of pipe tobacco, just like her father.

Tray was gaping like a fish and his eyes were as round as tree knots. Cather looked like someone had just done something embarrassing, and she didn't know whether to say something or keep quiet.

Mayten cleared her throat. "You'll have to excuse us, Your Majesty. We . . . this is Tray Traveler, Cather Healer, and I'm Mayten Singer."

"The singer! Excellent!"

Mayten heard giggles in the shadows beyond the door arch. The king's face grew dark. "Who's listening at my door?"

He crossed to the door in three giant steps. Cather took Mayten's hand as the king disappeared through the arch with a roar. Horrible shrieks echoed in the hall, sending chills down to Mayten's spine.

Were they standing in the castle of a crazy man?

Her body tensed but before she could move, the king came back, carrying a little girl—one in a yellow dress, one in green— under each arm with a smaller boy perched on his shoulders. Another boy clung to his leg, making him walk with a strange swinging gate. All four were laughing wildly.

The king stopped in front of them, swinging the two girls to the floor. "These are my lovely daughters, Thomasina Three and Thomasina Four, though don't ask me which is which."

The girls—with identical jet-black hair, long noses dusted with freckles, and dirty bare feet—gave little curtsies and beamed up at Mayten.

"You can call me Lemmy," said the one in the yellow dress.

"You can call me Limey," said the one in green.

"And this," said the king, peeling the boy off his leg and setting him on the floor, "is Thomas the Third."

The little boy giggled. "Father, I'm the second, not the third." He looked shyly up. "I'm called Blue."

Blue looked like his father, but with improbable rust-red hair and freckles. A completely different color of red than Hunter's had been. He looked to be Wollemi's age.

"Oh, so sorry. Of course, Thomas the Second." The king plucked the boy—smallest of all—off his neck and placed him on the floor next to his brother. "And what number Thomas are you?"

The little one had his black hair tied back in a braid. He glanced at them through long, thick lashes and held up three fingers while shoving two of his other hand into his mouth.

"Thomas the Third it is," the king said, placing a hand the size of a dinner plate on the small boy's head. "He is also known around the castle as Raz."

He gestured at the children. "They were excited to meet the fabled singer. Children, this is the person we've all been waiting for—Mayten Singer!"

Mayten's face heated. The king must have her confused with her mother. Mayten hadn't even completed her training. She wasn't anyone special.

Besides, didn't the castle have singers of its own?

Before she could voice the question, the children shouted and Mayten was almost knocked off her feet by four sets of arms being thrown around her waist and legs. She looked at her friends, wondering what on earth these children thought she could do.

CHAPTER TWENTY

"All right, all right." The king peeled the children off Mayten. "You'll have plenty of time to talk to her at dinner. Let's let the poor girl unpack at least."

"Father, I—" A tall boy walked into the room. Dressed in brilliant white trousers, knee-high boots, and a billowing blue shirt left open at the collar, Mayten almost didn't recognize the rider from the pond.

"Oh, you're here." He'd cleaned up, his wild hair slicked back and held in a tie at the nape of his neck. He looked stiff and uncomfortable.

"Don't you look fine, Thomas!" boomed the king. "Can't say I've ever seen you look quite so . . . Of course, it's not often we get visited by two beautiful women on the same day."

This surly boy must be Thomas the First.

The boy frowned, his face coloring slightly.

"You've met my oldest son?" the king asked, confirming her suspicion.

Tray gave a small bow, taking a step closer to Cather who managed a curtsy. Mayten tried to follow her lead, but one leg wobbled and she shifted into a bow. Where had Cather learned such a skill? No one curtsied in their village, not even to the clan leader.

Besides, this young man wasn't worth the effort of trying.

Such a strange king, Mayten thought, though she felt much kindlier toward the king than she did toward his oldest son.

Thomas the First—was he a prince, then?—bowed deeply. "Singer, Healer, Traveler," he said in a formal voice. "Welcome."

Mayten could feel a snarl begin to curl her lip. With effort, she made her face relax. *Gracious host, my foot.* This boy was no prince, not in her mind. Princes did not leer at people the way he'd leered at them back at the pond.

"Thomas, show our guests to their rooms if you would." The king smiled at them and offered a small bow. "I've had clean clothes laid out for you and arranged for small snacks. The benefit of having seven children is that there are always spare clothes around, though food often mysteriously disappears."

Seven children. Something else to remind her of home. Had the king and queen lost any of their children to the great fever like her family had?

The prince leaned in and whispered to his father.

"Eight! Of course!" The king grinned. "I forgot the most recent addition to our family. Another girl." He sighed, though the sound was happy. "This one took a lot from my wife, though. Could you look in on her, Healer? After you've changed and refreshed yourself, of course. She's having trouble regaining her strength. Thomas will show you the way."

"I'd be happy to, King Redmond." Cather's cheeks reddened.

"I'll go check on her now then. I'll see you shortly." The king strode from the room, whistling a tune as he left.

His presence had taken up so much of the room Mayten felt his leaving like a physical loss. The room grew quiet, the three of them staring at the prince who seemed to deflate.

"Come on, I'll show you to your rooms." He looked re-signed, though not eager. "Can I get your bags?"

"We're carrying everything we brought," Tray said.

The prince's expression changed slightly, though Mayten couldn't decide if he was impressed or disgusted. "Follow me then."

He led the way, falling into step with Tray. They were part-way down the hall when the prince began peppering Tray with questions—about questing.

Mayten and Cather glanced through the arched doorways as they walked. One room looked like a large nursery with sev-eral cribs and hand-carved toys littering the floor. Several doors were closed and Mayten found herself wondering what was in those rooms.

One open archway led to a dining room dominated by a long wooden table. From the loud banging and muffled shout-ing Mayten heard, she guessed there was a kitchen beyond the dining room and pictured people scurrying to prepare food for unexpected guests.

Her stomach grumbled. It had been some time since they'd eaten a proper meal.

While the downstairs had stone floors and smelled of food preparation, the stairs to the second floor were covered in a thick red carpet, worn but still beautiful. This fit Mayten's im-age of what a palace should look like.

The carpet led them to the second floor, softening their foot-steps and filling the air with comfort and welcome. Large open windows flooded the rooms with light and fresh air. Mayten loved the feel of the carpet under her boots. Her house had a few rugs over the wooden floor but to have the entire floor cov-ered in carpet felt like something of a dream. She longed to take off her boots and dig her toes into the soft carpet.

A sitting area topped the stairs. Small couches huddled beneath windows that looked out to sea. Books were scattered here and there, as if waiting for the next person to curl up and begin reading.

Mayten thought she'd love to sit by a window and read. It would be almost as nice as sitting on her tree branch with a good book.

Two hallways led away from the sitting room toward the rear of the castle. She'd misjudged the size of the building. It stretched much further back than it appeared, reminding her of the wings behind her own house. The wings of the homestead were visible from the front, fanning from the main building at an angle. These 'wings' stretched directly behind the castle.

Prince Thomas led them down the hall on the left.

"Do you think the family lives there?" Cather whispered, pointing to the hall to the right.

"Perhaps," Mayten said. "Or maybe they have rooms on the main floor. These wings could be for guests. Maybe we'll get a chance to explore."

Thomas gestured to the first door on his right. "Traveler, this is your room." He gestured to the first two rooms on the left. "Singer and Healer, your rooms are here. They have an adjoining door. I'll let you decide who sleeps where. Healer, would you join me by the stairs as soon as you've changed? I'll take you to my mother."

Cather nodded, looking more shy than normal. Had she become smitten with this strange prince? Mayten glanced at Tray, who didn't look happy.

"I'll see the rest of you at dinner. You'll hear a bell to call you." He turned and hurried away without giving Mayten a second look.

Good, I might have had to punch him.

"Three rooms," Cather said, "all to ourselves."

The thought of not sharing a room with her cranky sister made Mayten smile.

Cather pointed down the hall. Doors lined the hall on both sides. "I wonder if anyone else is staying here?"

Tray opened his door and the girls followed him in. The small room had a bed under the window which Tray quickly jumped on, boots and all. It was not like Mayten's bed at home, framed in rich cherry wood, but a slender mattress stuffed with cotton over a rope woven frame. After sleeping on the ground, even a thin mattress would feel like heaven. There was a tray of bread and cheese next to his bed and he began cramming large pieces of both into his mouth.

Mayten rolled her eyes. "We are in a castle, Tray. You could try not to eat like a pig."

He shrugged and kept eating.

"I can't tell you how happy I am to be sleeping in a real bed tonight," he said around his food. He stretched like a cat on the bed. The room smelled like lemons with a touch of briny air from the open window. The lowering sun bathed the room in a warm glow.

Mayten leaned out the open window, smiling at the gardens below. A quick look toward the pond told her what she wanted to know. "You can't see the pond from here. That row of trees shelters it."

A soft snore drew her attention. Tray was already asleep. Evidently, having to act like a responsible adult had been exhausting for him.

"I'm glad to hear that," Cather said. "Why don't we take a look at our rooms? I have to change and meet the prince."

She grabbed Mayten by the hand and pulled her into the hall, gently closing Tray's door behind them.

The next room was larger than Tray's and connected to the room beyond through an open door. Mayten could see enough of the other room to tell the bed was similar to the bed in this room. Both beds were easily twice the size of Tray's.

"Look at this dress!" Cather lifted a flowing pink gown from the bed. "It might be a bit too long but it's beautiful!"

Mayten nodded. "It's perfect for you. The color goes great with your eyes."

She wandered the room, admiring the paintings of flowers set above a vase filled with fresh flowers that mimicked the painting's lilies. She resisted the urge to pick up the Caspian figurines on the low table, deciding the fancy boxes sitting next to the figurines weren't as fragile. She opened the lid of one box, delighted to hear music start playing.

The room had a fireplace and a bathtub like the one her family had bought. The bathtub crouched on a platform in front of a second window and was easily twice the size of the bath her family owned.

A full-length mirror stood next to the dressing table. The mirror's wood frame swiveled when she touched it, swinging easily toward her . . .

"Wonder what I looked like before our little bath," she snorted, feeling heat creep into her face.

"Why don't you check the other room?" Cather asked. "There's probably another dress in there."

The other room had no bath and no fireplace, only a large bed with a wide window that faced the tall thin trees they had seen earlier that offered privacy to the castle. A chair with a table holding a small stack of books and an oil lamp sat by the window.

"I'll take this room," Mayten said. She reached for a book but a shriek from Cather pulled her around.

"Another beautiful dress!" Cather held up an emerald green dress that shimmered in the late afternoon sun. Mayten had to admit the dress was beautiful, though secretly she'd hoped to find pants she could wear.

"This dress will look fantastic with your hair." Cather turned the dress around. "Look at the scooped collar and the buttons up the back . . . But wouldn't you like the bigger room?"

"No," Mayten said, "this room is perfect for me, but thanks. I will share the bathtub, though. And—it is all right to leave the door open? I've gotten used to having you so close by."

Cather nodded. "I feel like Tray is miles away and he's only across the hall. I guess living together has made us like a family."

She grinned at Mayten as she yanked her tunic over her head. "Help me with this dress?"

Mayten held the pink dress high so Cather could find her way through the skirts, then pulled the dress down and helped fasten buttons. Lots of pearl buttons.

Cather handed Mayten a brush from the dressing table, carefully sitting on a chair that looked like it might break beneath a larger person's weight. Mayten worked the tangles from Cather's wavy hair.

When she was done, Cather stood and turned to the mirror.

They both gasped. The dress hugged Cather's shoulders, draping her body in soft folds. Brown wavy hair cascaded down her back.

"Beautiful!" Mayten couldn't believe the change in her friend. She felt drab next to her, like a moth next to a butterfly. "Tray'd better be careful or that prince will try and steal you away."

"I think the prince is handsome, don't you?" Cather raised an eyebrow, glancing at Mayten in the mirror as she turned from side to side, studying her image critically.

Mayten frowned. "When he frowns, which is often, the space between his eyebrows completely disappears like he has one long eyebrow. And don't even get me started on his nose."

Cather was always trying to interest her in different boys and was disappointed when Mayten showed no interest. She laughed, shaking her head, then turned and hugged Mayten tight.

Mayten's eyes burned as she returned the hug. Something was happening to her friend, though Mayten didn't have the words for it.

"I'd better go," Cather said, pulling free. "I don't think it's proper to keep a prince waiting."

A sense of loss filled Mayten. Cather was being swept along the river of life, leaving Mayten alone on the shore.

CHAPTER TWENTY-ONE

Instead of exploring the books on the table, Mayten sat in the chair next to the window—a chair big enough to hold her da and half her siblings—and passed the time digging through her mother's book, looking for clues about communicating with another person using the trees.

After what seemed like hours of looking and finding nothing helpful, she glanced at the other books. A cover showing a dragon fighting a knight caught her eye.

The books at home were worn to threads, having been read over and over by all the children. Her parents bought books from traders whenever they could, but Mayten always wanted more.

Was it possible to borrow some books to take home? Would it be improper to ask a king if she could borrow a few books?

And when would she be able to get the books back to him?

She tucked her feet under her and fell into a beautifully illustrated story about knights, princesses, and dragons. The knights had the most fun, she decided as she nibbled on a piece of dark brown bread.

A bell rang during a rather intense fight scene, shocking her back to reality.

Mayten jumped to her feet, staring in dismay at her clothes. She tugged off her boots, pants, and shirt, yanked the dress over her head, and dug her sandals from her pack. She hopped toward the door, pulling her sandals on and trying to button the back of her dress at the same time. She almost collided with Tray in the hall, his eyes still bleary from sleep. His hair stuck up at odd angles.

"Button me, quick!"

"Huh?"

She turned her back, pointing to the buttons, trying not to fuss as he fumbled to fasten them.

"Funny, I thought you'd go for the pretty one, Tray."

The voice behind her was familiar and unwelcome.

Adven.

Anger boiled in Mayten's belly. Her face flushed with heat, and she had to stop herself from snapping back. She'd promised Hunter she would try to see the good in their leader—

"Uncle!" Tray's face lit up. "How'd you get here so fast?"

He left her standing in the hall with a half-buttoned dress, following Adven to the stairs. Tray not only looked fully awake, he appeared to be greatly relieved.

"I can move fast when I'm alone."

"Excuse me, Miss."

Mayten started, jerking back from an older man who had appeared next to her. This man was as round as the secretary, though much shorter. He had a receding hairline that ended in a nest of gray curls and a pleasant, grandfatherly way about him.

"I am Count Monroe," he said with a slight bow and a smile that put Mayten at ease. "I mean no disrespect, but may I offer my assistance with those buttons?"

Was it proper to let a strange man button her dress?

More proper than going to dinner half-dressed, she decided. She turned her back to him, moving her braids out of the way. "Thank you, sir."

The dress was buttoned in no time. She turned to thank him again, pleasantly surprised by the deliciously fresh smell—a smell that brought oranges to mind—that seemed to surround him.

The count reminded her of someone—was it her da's father? He'd died of the wasting sickness when she was only five, but she'd had a great fondness for the old man. She'd sat on his lap while he read to her, feeling warm and safe. He'd loved to read and had passed that love on to her.

"Thank you so much. I'm afraid I was in a bit of a pickle. I'm Mayten."

"My pleasure. It's been a while since I've had the opportunity to help any maidens in distress." The count hooked his walking stick over his right arm and offered her his left. She slipped her hand beneath his crooked elbow and let him lead her to the stairs.

Mayten wondered if he'd been a friend of her grandfather's. "Have you ever visited the forest clan?"

"Once, briefly. I stopped by on a trading barge. But I'm sure it was before you were born, child," he said with a chuckle. "It was a magnificent place to watch furniture in the making, boats too. They used the most beautiful wood."

She smiled at the compliment. "They still do. My mother manages the forest there. She's a tree singer and has a great relationship with the forest."

He chuckled again. "Ah, you must be the fabled singer who has come to rescue us!"

His eyes sparkled and she wondered if he found the idea as silly and incomprehensible as she.

Mayten stopped and lowered her voice. "People keep saying that, sir, but I don't know why. Don't they have any singers here?"

"Oh no, my dear. There hasn't been a singer in the castle for ages."

"But why not?"

He seemed to draw into himself, as if he wanted to tell her something but didn't know if he should. He turned back to the stairs and led her downward. "I'm sure you'll hear about it soon enough, *but* . . . I've always had a fondness for singers. Perhaps someday I'll have the privilege to visit your clan again. I would love to meet your mother."

She let him guide her down the stairs, her mind on his last words.

But—he'd said the word as though some folks did *not* have a fondness for singers, a fact she'd recently learned firsthand. Yet, everyone she'd met at the castle seemed to think she was something special.

Mayten shrugged. There'd likely be time to work it out later. She was about to dine in a castle. She had made it this far. She could worry about the rest later.

Adven and Tray had already disappeared down the stairs, and she was thankful she didn't have to enter the dining room alone. When they reached the bottom of the stairs, the count led her into the room with the exceptionally long table. Candles in wall sconces lit the room in a gentle glow. Tapestries hung on every wall. A beautiful meadow scene with a flowing river and a family of deer in the foreground caught her attention right off.

Tray and Adven were still standing. The king sat at the far end, an empty chair to his right. The queen's chair, she guessed.

The children were seated around the table in what seemed a random order with the prince to the king's left. Cather sat next to him, blushing, which likely was the reason for the scowl on Tray's face.

Two older girls—daughters she hadn't yet met—sat next to Cather. Was she wearing one of their castoffs?

Everyone looked up with smiles when she entered, the king and the prince rising as though one. Adven and Tray turned as well.

Had the queen arrived then?

Mayten glanced over her shoulder, but no one was there.

CHAPTER TWENTY-TWO

Mayten stood at the entrance of the dining room with Count Monroe. The large table was beautifully set with more matching dishes than she had ever seen. The table at home was almost as long but their dishes were a mishmash collected over the years from trading ships.

The four younger children were scrubbed and dressed in crisp white shirts, the boys in short pants and the girls in skirts. The king and three elder children were decked out in rich warm colors with the girls in velvet dresses and the men in matching black vests.

Their team must look bedraggled after such a long trek, a hasty dip in the lake, and wearing hand-me-down clothes.

The smells coming from the kitchen made her stomach growl and she eyed the bowls of bread and plates of cheeses.

"Mayten Singer," the king's voice made the room seem small. He gestured at the empty chair beside him. "Please join me."

Shock made her shiver. Why was she being honored in this way? She glanced at Cather. Her friend lifted her eyebrows and gave a slight shrug.

"Count, would you mind taking the queen's place?" The king nodded at the chair at the end of the table.

"I'd be happy to." The count gave a short bow.

"Travelers, if you please," the king continued. "Find a place to sit, though I must warn you—the younger children may need help cutting their meat."

Thankfully, the count escorted Mayten to her seat, giving her a deeper bow before excusing himself and taking his own seat.

The four younger children were not seated randomly but spaced so that adults were nearby to help them. She caught Adven patting the hair of the second littlest Thomas, the one who reminded her of Wollemi. Something in the unexpected gesture tightened her throat.

Odd that he could be kind to others, but not to her.

Sir Underbrush skidded into the room, overstuffed and breathless. He'd changed into looser pants and a more casual shirt. "Sorry I'm late, Tom, er . . . Your Majesty."

He glanced nervously around the table, wincing when he noticed the only seat available was nestled between a pair of talkative girls, the twins.

"Nonsense, Thornton," the king said. "Have a seat and cut the 'Majesty' codswallop, will you?"

Sir Underbrush bobbed his head and took his seat between the girls . . . who immediately started talking over each other, their conversation involving some new kittens that had been born. He looked from one to the other and back again as if trying to keep up with the conversation.

Mayten hid a smile.

She had expected to find a stodgy old man sitting on the throne. This king was neither stodgy nor old. She loved the way he included his children at the evening meal when he could have put them in a separate room to eat. He didn't act like a king at all—at least not like the kings she'd read about.

And Sir Underbrush played the court jester perfectly, intentional or not.

King Redmond gestured at the oldest girls. "You haven't met my two eldest gems yet. This is the oldest, Thomasina," he gestured at the daughter with straight hair the same rust-red color as the king's beard, the same color as little Blue's. Thomasina's features and skin color resembled the king's, but on her, those features looked feminine and soft. "Everyone here at the castle calls her Cherry."

Mayten nodded at the girl. "It's nice to meet you."

"Cherry has recently accepted the proposal of a lad from your neck of the woods," the king continued. "He's from the Ocean Clan; the captain of a ship. They plan to sail the seas and have lots of adventures."

The king's eyes glistened, and his daughter beamed back at him. Mayten could see the love in the king's eyes, and it made her heart ache for her own da.

"I have two sisters that live with the Ocean Clan," Mayten said. "I'll tell you their names so you can have someone to welcome you!"

Cherry smiled at her. "Thank you. It will be hard to live so far from home."

The king cleared his throat. "And this lovely maid is Thomasina Two, also known as Nan."

Mayten looked at the king's second oldest daughter, the word 'homely' immediately popping into her mind. The girl had large front teeth and a bit of an overbite along with the same long straight nose and thick brows as her brother Thomas. The features were even less becoming on her.

Thomasina Two did not smile at Mayten. In fact, she was the only one of the king's children not smiling—*if* Mayten ignored the prince.

"Nan here is studying botany and is the artist responsible for all of the amazing shrubberies you see around the grounds." The king beamed at his daughter with evident pride.

Nan blushed and dipped her head.

"The bushes are lovely," Cather said.

Nan gave her a shy smile.

"They *are* beautiful," Mayten said, nodding her head in agreement.

Nan's smile faded. She dipped her head in a tight-lipped nod and turned to her sister.

What on earth had she done now? Mayten had just met the girl, yet somehow, she'd already managed to offend her. She glanced around the table clockwise. She sat next to the king. Then there were Cherry and Nan. Next to them the twins, Lemmy and Limey, with the mystified Sir Underbrush between them.

Near the end of the table sat Blue, the little one who reminded her of Wollemi. Adven sat next to him, seeming to listen to the boy's every word.

Count Monroe was at the far end, smiling happily at little Raz. Tray was between Raz and Cather. Mayten noticed that he was keeping a close eye on Cather who also sat next to the prince.

No one seemed aware that Nan had glowered at her.

The king reached for his glass—filled partway with what appeared to be red wine—and raised it high, his children quickly following suit, though the younger children's glasses appeared to be filled with milk.

Mayten stared at the table set with plates, more forks than she knew what to do with, and two glasses at each place. She glanced at the prince who sat to her right. He was also holding a wine glass.

She grabbed the glass and lifted it. She'd had wine at holidays and never really cared for it. Would she be able to actually drink the stuff without choking?

"To our guests!" the king said, his voice ringing throughout the room. "May your stay in our home be restful, may you sleep deeply and well, and may you each take one child when you leave!"

With a hearty bellow, the king lifted his glass to his lips. The children let out a chorus of protests and groans.

"I'll take this one," Adven said with a grin. He ruffled Blue's hair again.

Mayten frowned, then quickly smoothed her expression. Why did he have to go and choose the boy she liked best?

The king studied Blue. "Number two, is it? Well, now, I don't know." He stroked his beard.

Little Blue's lip quivered. Did he really think his father might actually send him off with Adven? Poor thing—

"No, Traveler. I've grown a bit fond of Number Two."

The little boy let out a breath and smiled.

The king glanced around the table. "Matter of fact, it appears I've become attached to them all. Maybe that new one . . . what was her name?"

Blue looked up, a crease furrowing his forehead. "Father, how can you forget her name? It's Thomasina Five, little Plumb! And you can't give her away. She's my favorite!"

A chorus of laughter rose from the table. The children didn't realize the king was joking—they all called out in protest, distraught over the idea of losing their baby sister. The twins started to whimper.

All at once, Mayten felt an urge to be somewhere else. The noise was overwhelming, sound echoing off the stone walls.

"Okay, okay." The king raised his arms in surrender. "I promise I'll keep you all. Except Prince Thomas."

The children quieted, though their eyes grew large and round. The king raised a bushy eyebrow at his eldest son. "I'm afraid Thomas here has been bitten by the bug of adventure. Being a prince isn't enough for him anymore. He would rather join a quest."

The king turned to Adven. "Would you consider taking him with you?"

Something in the king's demeanor led Mayten to believe the question was not really a question but a kindly worded demand.

The prince's dour expression turned hopeful as he looked at Adven, waiting for a reply.

What would Adven think of taking a prince on a quest? Especially a spoiled, haughty one? He'd been reluctant enough to bring her and Cather along.

Adven sipped his wine and regarded the prince. Mayten jumped as Adven slammed his wine glass on the table. "Of course!"

The children erupted in cheers.

Adven raised a hand and they immediately quieted. "As long as I'm not responsible if he gets eaten by a bear, mauled by a mountain lion, or gored by the tusks of a wild boar."

Mayten's throat clenched as visions of Hunter lying still on the ground flooded her mind.

The children all protested at once, determined their beloved brother wouldn't be eaten by a bear. The prince's jaw clenched. Was he afraid his father would change his mind?

Again, the king raised his hands and the children quieted. Judging by the serious look in his eyes, this man knew what had happened to their woodsman. He was also aware of the very real dangers his son might encounter. "I trust you will do everything in your power to protect the prince. That said, if something out of your control were to happen, I would not hold you responsible."

The prince grinned so wide it seemed his face might split. A thrill ran down Mayten's back. When he smiled, he was almost handsome with the same charming space between his front teeth his father had. He should try smiling more often.

Adven lifted his glass to the king in acknowledgment, but she knew him well enough by now to see that his smile did not reach his eye.

"Now that that's settled," the king clapped his hands, "let's eat!"

The door behind him burst open and servants streamed in, bearing heaping platters of meat, fruits, and vegetables. Mayten's mouth watered. The sight of fresh fruits and vegetables made her heart glad and her stomach growl.

Save for the clinking of glasses and the scraping of fork against plate, the room fell silent. Mayten lost all of her nervousness about which fork to use for what and ate until she could eat no more.

She sat back in her seat with a sigh just as the king tapped his spoon on his water glass. "Friends, I've promised the young ones an opportunity to ask one question of each of our visitors before they must go off to bed. Who will go first?"

All four little ones waved their arms in the air with a chorus of "pick me!" and "I will."

The king held up his hand, and they quieted. "We'll go by age. Thomasina the Third, Lemmy. You'll go first."

The twin to Sir Underbrush's right didn't hesitate. "We heard you came with a dog!" she said to Mayten. "What's his name? Can we play with him?"

The king laughed. "Just like you to sneak in extra questions, Number Three." He turned to Mayten. "I had the opportunity to meet your canine friend earlier. He is quite an impressive fellow and seems gentle. Some sort of mastiff, is he?"

"That's what the trader said." Mayten nodded. "He was a puppy when we got him, and we had no idea how big he would grow."

"Is it all right with you if the children play with him in the morning?"

"Of course," Mayten said. The king seemed aware of everything going on in his castle. "His name is Anatolian, and he is great with children. I have brothers and sisters too, and I'm sure he misses them."

The children cheered.

The king opened his hand to Limey, the younger of the twins, who turned to Mayten as the rest quieted. "Are you really a singer? How did you get to be one? Can you teach me to be one?"

Her father laughed. "You two are stretching the rules! But I know you've been waiting to ask Mayten about her ability to sing to trees ever since you heard she was coming." His face grew serious. "We've never met a singer before. What can you tell us?"

Why didn't the castle have singers? she wondered again. Her face grew warm as all eyes turned toward her . . . and not all the eyes were friendly.

Where on earth should she start?

"In our clan," the eager smiles of the children set her more at ease, "we each receive a calling when we turn fifteen. I was called to be a tree singer . . . I'm from a family of singers . . ."

She thought a moment. "And a quester, for now anyway. In our clan, questers are held in high esteem, as are healers. Singers aren't thought of as anything special."

Adven coughed.

She scowled at him and continued. "Most people are called to be what their parents were, but occasionally someone from outside is called to be a singer or healer."

The children watched her with rapt attention, their faces lit, eyes shining.

Mayten couldn't stand it any longer. "But please, Your Majesty, why doesn't your clan have any singers?"

The king shifted, stroking his beard. "That's a long story for another time. Let's hear more about singers. I believe Limey asked if singing was something you could teach?"

Mayten swallowed her questions and continued. All four children were curious about her singing and she talked until the king clapped his hands and sent the young ones to bed.

Why had the king dodged her question? she wondered as the children filed out. Surely the western forests needed the management of singers. Singers saw to the health of the forest, and the king's forests were vast.

No wonder the blight started here.

This was it, Mayten realized. The first piece of the puzzle. If she could find out what happened to the castle's singers, she'd know why the blight was spreading.

CHAPTER TWENTY-THREE

After dinner, women wearing white aprons over their dresses came to collect the younger children. Mayten assumed they were the children's nannies, taking them off to prepare for bed. King Redmond led the rest of them down the hall to the room where he had greeted them earlier.

"To strategize," he said when the prince asked why they were back in the library.

Finally, Mayten would find out exactly why they were here. Her heart leaped when Anatolian loped in followed by the young boy Sir Underbrush had sent him off with. The dog looked cleaner than she'd ever seen him and he smelled better too. Someone had tied a red triangle of scarf around his neck. Mayten bent to give him a good rubbing and he greeted her with a face wash of kisses.

"Come in, old boy. You're a part of this too." The king smiled and gave Anatolian a scratch.

A fire crackled in the fireplace, and the smell of pine and cinnamon warmed the air. The overstuffed chairs and couches had been drawn into a semi-circle around the fireplace.

And the books! Mayten could not get over so many books.

She'd be happy to stay here forever, she decided. Curled up by the fire, Anatolian at her feet, and a book in her hand. The castle had no singers; maybe she could be the first.

Cherry excused herself to check on the queen. Sir Underbrush excused himself as well. Like as not, the secretary was always attending to one thing or another, though she hadn't a clue as to what those 'things' might be.

That left the king, Nan—the daughter studying botany who seemed to have taken a dislike to Mayten—Prince Thomas, Cather, Tray, Adven, and Count Monroe. A surly looking man joined them at the last minute.

The surly man met her eyes and gooseflesh crawled up her arms. There was something familiar about his eyes, something haughty. And his scowl reminded her of Adven.

She didn't even know this man. Why would he—why would anyone—dislike her as soon as they met her?

Tray grabbed a seat next to Cather as everyone sat—or curled, in Mayten's case—in a chair or on a couch. The prince glanced at the pair with a scowl, then settled in a chair next to Mayten.

The king leaned forward, elbows on his knees. "I didn't want to frighten the little ones, but the situation with our forest is quite dire. Trees to the north of us are dying and we don't know why."

Nan sat next to her father. She pulled a notebook from the small table next to her chair. She flipped a few pages as though refreshing her memory, then gave a quick nod.

"I've run every test I can think of to determine the cause of the deaths. There are no beetles, no imbalance in the soil or weather to cause such a drastic change. But the trees *are* dying." Nan's voice was slightly nasal, as though she'd breathed too much dust.

"It's almost like they are standing, but empty of life. They are not hollow. I've had several cut down so that I could inspect them and there is no apparent rot or sign of drought or disease, but when a big windstorm comes in, they just fall over. They look perfectly healthy on the inside and the outside, but they fall over dead."

Mayten gasped. What would cause healthy trees to fall over like that?

She glanced at each member of the group in turn, wishing with all her heart that her mother had been the one sitting in this chair instead of her. Mother would know what to do, how to figure out what the problem was and how to solve it.

"We must figure out what is causing this before the winter storms come back," Nan continued. "Last winter we lost over one thousand trees."

One. Thousand. Trees.

Mayten could barely breathe. Her clan harvested about two hundred trees a year. She couldn't picture the loss of a thousand. Something like this could devastate a forest—an entire economy—in no time. Why hadn't they asked for help when they first noticed the problem?

"Of course, they weren't a total loss," Nan said with a shrug. "Father brought in loggers to salvage what they could, then ship the logs off to several ports, including yours." She nodded at Tray.

"Excuse me," Mayten said hesitantly. "I can't help but wonder if that was the best decision? What if the trees had some unknown sickness that might spread to the trees in the ports where they'd been shipped?"

"The wood was still good," Nan snapped. She turned back to Tray. "We built furniture and other items with the wood before exporting it. Everything has remained sound. Then we inspected each tree before it was shipped."

Her face flushed and her voice rose in pitch. "There is much more at stake here than the loss of the trees. The entire forest system will become imbalanced—if the trees die, the plants and insects that live in them will die, the birds and other small creatures that live off those insects will die, the larger animals that live off of those insects will die. The entire island, and possibly the entire world could become imbalanced, shifting the weather patterns and changing the seasons until we are all just a barren desert!"

The king laid a hand on his daughter's arm. "One thing at a time, Nan. One thing at a time."

Nan took a breath, crossed her arms, and leaned back in her chair. The storm boiling inside her showed on her face. Her eyebrows met in a seething glower, her face flushed red as though burned by the sun.

She's been carrying this burden too long. Though Mayten still had no idea *how* long. The girl was probably relieved to finally get some help.

"Nan tends to look on the dark side of things I'm afraid, " the king said with a sigh. "I'm sure the singer can help us figure this out."

Nan slapped her notebook closed and clamped her lips together, glaring at Mayten.

I guess I'm not the one she was hoping would come.

Where did all this animosity come from? Did the girl resent Mayten for being a singer? Perhaps—not having grown up around singers—she felt science should have revealed an answer. If that were the case, perhaps she also felt those gifted with a calling were nothing more than frauds performing magic tricks.

Though something the princess said stuck in Mayten's mind. She mulled the words over. Something about the seasons changing . . .

The oak tree she had last sat on had tried to show her that too. Just as the tree tried to show her that something threatened the very life of the forest—quite possibly all of their lives.

"Mayten," said the king, and from the sound of his voice, it wasn't the first time he'd tried to catch her attention.

"I'm sorry, King Redmond. What did you say?"

"I'd like your team to start out tomorrow, after the noon meal. Take the evening to rest up and restock your provisions. I'm sorry I can't let you rest longer. I don't imagine this will be a long quest—no more than a week or so. You should be able to at least get an idea about what is happening so we can make plans to correct it." He looked at her hopefully.

Suddenly the room felt less like a library and more like a room for a war council. Mayten nodded, struggling to look confident even though she was quivering like a raw egg inside.

How was she supposed to know if she could figure out what was happening in a week, let alone what they could do to fix it? The question weighed her down like a heavy blanket.

"Adven, you will lead the team, of course," the king continued. "If you don't mind, I'd like to keep Tray here and send Thomas in his place. I'd like my son to have a chance to see what a quest is like before he decides to join you on a longer adventure."

The prince grinned, that beautiful smile Mayten had seen only once before. He had the king's charm when he smiled like that, the gap between his front teeth visible again. For a moment, she could not look away.

Adven nodded, although she could tell by the set of his jaw he was not happy. She supposed there was only one way to reply when a king made a request.

Tray's wide eyes showed his shock and dismay. Mayten could tell he wanted to protest, but he clamped his mouth shut.

"Cather Healer, may I ask you to please stay with the queen?" the king asked. "She found your visit this afternoon quite comforting. With more time, perhaps you'll be able to discern the problem."

"Of course, Your Majesty," Cather said, dipping her head. Her dark hair glistened in the firelight.

She belonged in the castle, Mayten realized. Much more so than a ruffian who rushed to dinner half-dressed and didn't even know how to curtsy properly or which fork to use.

Tray's shoulders relaxed and a slight smile creased his face. He put his arm on the top of the couch above Cather's head, as if to claim his territory.

"Also, I'd like to have Nan join you. She has done a great deal of research that may be helpful to you." The king smiled at his daughter, a smile that Mayten didn't share.

Dread dragged at her stomach, churning the evening's lovely meal into heavy mud. *Might as well fill the entire team with I Hate Mayten members.*

Adven cleared his throat. "King Thomas, we've lost our woodsman—" His voice broke.

Mayten's eyes burned at the mention of their lost teammate.

"Of course." The king raised his hand apologetically. "I heard of your loss and am deeply sorry for it. One of our best woodsmen has volunteered to accompany you."

He turned to the one person Mayten didn't yet know. "This is Rafe."

The surly man dipped his head.

Adven nodded back.

Two grumpy peas in a pod. This trip gets more fun by the second.

"Thank you, sire," Adven said, his manner stiff as a fireplace poker.

"And Count Monroe." The king nodded at the older gentleman sitting next to Nan. "The count is a respected historian. He's traveled far and wide and knows more about these lands, on a historical level, than anyone I've ever met. He might be of particular help to you, Mayten. He has asked to go along, and I have granted his wish."

Mayten breathed a sigh of relief, but Adven's eyes darkened. He likely thought the older man would slow them down, but she didn't mind. At least there would be one person who didn't hate her along with them.

A quester who hated singers, a prince who would prefer the company of her best friend, a scientist who thought—who knew what Nan thought?—and a scary-looking woodsman. What could possibly go wrong?

She glanced at Count Monroe, and he gave her a reassuring smile. It helped a little, but she doubted she'd be getting any sleep tonight.

CHAPTER TWENTY-FOUR

Contrary to Mayten's fears, she slept deeply in the soft bed, Anatolian on the woven rug on the floor next to her, so deeply she didn't wake until the breakfast bell rang.

She yanked on her borrowed dress as she dashed down the stairs, Anatolian at her heels. Edward was waiting for her at the bottom of the stairs, calling Anatolian outside as she hurried into the dining room. Cather showed up a moment later, looking just as rushed and harried as Mayten felt, her hair billowing in a disheveled cloud around her.

The same group gathered together for breakfast. Still no sign of the queen.

The children were so excited to get to play with Anatolian that they raced through the meal. Mayten's stomach was too bound up in knots to eat much even though the cooked oats and fruit looked delicious. As she started to get up and retrieve the dog, the king touched her sleeve.

"I'm wondering, Mayten, if we might walk a bit in the garden before you start your packing? Edward can get Anatolian for the children when they're done eating."

"Of course," she said, curious to hear what the king had to say. Perhaps she'd figure out a way to get more information from him before they departed—like the story about what happened to their last singer.

She followed him out of the dining room and down the long hall, turning into a wide doorway that led to the kitchen.

"I hope you don't mind taking a shortcut," he said, voice raised above the kitchen noise. "As you can tell, I'm not one to stand on ceremony."

"Not at all," she said, looking around at the bustling staff. The chaos reminded her of home, though this kitchen looked nothing like her da's kitchen.

They stood at one end of a large room with a table running down the middle. Large pots and ladles hung along the walls and a huge fire burned in the fireplace against the far wall. The pots were made of gleaming brass, covering the walls like beautiful artwork.

The king led her along one side, then slipped out a side door leading into the gardens. They walked in silence, her ears ringing after the noisy kitchen. The sandy path crunched softly with each step and she found herself admiring flower beds luxurious with spring flowers of fuchsia and red intermixed with the enormous ornamental bushes she had seen from the lake.

The air had a bit of a nip, but the sun was up, and a sweet aroma filled the air. Up close, the garden's beauty took her breath away. There were plants she'd never seen and she committed them to memory, determined to tell her da every detail when she got home.

The king walked silently next to her seeming to sense her need to take it all in. It was the quietest she had seen the man.

"I'm sorry," she finally said. "You wanted to talk to me, and here I am gawking at the garden. I've never seen anything like it in my life and my da is a master gardener. He would love to see this."

The king smiled. "It's all Nan. She has quite an eye for color and a way of making things grow. Her mother is like that too. At least she was . . . before she got sick. Perhaps your father could come someday. We'd love to have him visit."

"He would enjoy that." She could picture her da sniffing, digging, *tasting* the dirt. He would be in his element—

"Yesterday you asked why we have no singers. I wanted to give you the full story, before you heard gossip from those who don't really know. This story was handed down from my father and grandfather. Yes, it has grown over time and become large as legend, but it is the most accurate answer I can give you."

Mayten stiffened, unsure what to expect.

The king clasped his hands behind his back and paced back and forth in front of her on the path. "Singers were held in high esteem back in my great-grandfather's day. When my grandfather was but a boy, however, one of our singers went bad."

Mayten's head whirled, then stuck, like a saw blade jammed in a tree. "Went *bad*? Whatever do you mean?"

"The details are a bit sketchy, but it is my understanding that a singer can sing life into something, is that true?"

"Not exactly," Mayten said, struggling to think clearly. "Every living thing has life in it—its life energy. A singer can encourage that life to expand, making it healthier, directing its growth."

She paused, then continued. "In much the same way Nan directs the growth of these hedges with hedge trimmers, singers direct energy into the growth of the trees and plants, through our songs. But it's more than that. We listen to them too. We form a . . . relationship with the trees."

She'd never tried to explain her calling to someone who had no idea what she was talking about.

"I see." The king plucked a large red star-shaped flower and handed it to Mayten. She smiled her thanks.

Da grew these, amaryllis. She tucked the flower into her braid behind her ear. He was quiet as he turned and led her further down the path.

After a few moments, he continued his story. "As I understand it, this singer found a way to take the energy *from* the plants instead of giving them energy—or encouraging the plants to grow as you described, though I'm not certain I quite understand."

Once again, nausea churned Mayten's stomach. Taking energy from a plant was unthinkable. The very idea made her want to vomit.

Every child, when they were first learning to sing, made the mistake of taking too much energy from a plant. Of course, the plant died—which was why children practiced on weeds. They were soundly chastised when that happened and made to watch. Feeling a plant die usually hurt enough to make the children more careful.

It was a dark and painful feeling, like all the joy had been sucked from the world, an experience not easily forgotten.

She couldn't imagine a singer ever doing such a harmful thing on purpose, and Mother had never mentioned any such incident. Singers were connected to the earth in a healing way. That kind of destruction went against everything she had ever learned.

It wasn't just wrong. It was evil.

"He became quite powerful," the king continued, "but something about the experience of taking from the plants also twisted his mind."

Was this the man the trees had shown to her? The man they had not forgiven?

"He began taking power from other living creatures. When he was found next to the dead body of my grandfather's favorite dog, my great-grandfather exiled him from the kingdom, issuing a proclamation. Singers were no longer allowed in the castle. Unfortunately, he also forbade anyone from talking about the matter which, I'm sorry to say, has created some superstitions around singers here at Trigginsfeld."

Mayten spotted a bench and hurried over to it, her knees collapsing as she felt cold stone press against her legs. She rested her head in her hands, willing the garden to stop spinning. *This is why there was no telling of this story in the clan's memory.*

The king took her hand and patted it. "My apologies. I didn't mean to distress you."

"I . . . I just . . . need a minute."

"I assure you, I have done my best to dispel that black mark on the reputation of singers. I've forbidden my staff to speak ill of singers and, as you can see, my children hold them in the highest esteem. A history of faithfulness does not need to be dismissed because of one dangerous man."

Mayten nodded. She could not rid her mind of the image of his grandfather's dog—a dog like Anatolian—lying dead on the ground.

She had never heard of anyone taking energy from an animal, not even an insect. The very idea made her skin crawl. Singers were healers of plants, not murderers.

"I wanted you to hear the story from me." The king straightened, his face gone even more serious. "I also want to offer you a position at the castle when you have finished your training. I think enough time has passed. The edict against singers needs to be—and shall be—revoked."

A shudder ran through Mayten's body. She gulped for air, afraid she might faint right in front of the king.

Had he just said he wanted her to be the castle singer?

Yes, she'd thought about that very thing last night. But it had only been a daydream. How could she leave her family? They'd been gone barely two weeks and she'd spent half the time longing for home.

"As you can see," the king continued, holding out a hand. Mayten took his warm fingers, willing herself to her feet. "The castle needs singers. It is my fervent hope you will come back and bring a younger singer or two with you. They should be trained here with at least one of my children. And of course, they should be trained by the best singer on the island."

The best? She'd done nothing to prove herself yet. What if she just wanted to stay on the homestead as she'd dreamed before coming to the castle?

Could someone say no to a king?

She took a deep breath, trying to slow her heart. "Your Majesty, I am delighted that you want singers to be represented in the castle. Just now, I'm feeling a bit overwhelmed by the task set before me. Would it be okay if we see how this quest goes before I make any long-term plans?"

The king laughed, the twinkle returning to his eyes. He patted her arm. "That, my dear, was the most diplomatic way anyone has ever told me to slow down!"

The pressure around Mayten's ribs eased. He didn't seem angry at her suggestion.

"We will see how the quest goes. I have complete faith that you will figure out what is causing our current crisis. Now, let's get back so you can pack. I've had all your clothes washed and they should be ready to wear." He chuckled and shook his head as he led her back in through the kitchen. "I must tell you, however, that a king generally gets whatever a king wants."

CHAPTER TWENTY-FIVE

Mayten and Cather stood in their room in the castle while Mayten packed for the quest. The king had said it would be a fact-finding trip and only take about a week, so she didn't want to carry too much.

"I'm going to miss you." Mayten sighed as Cather helped her pack. "And I only got a quick soak in that tub. I didn't even get to explore the castle. Do try to explore it while I'm gone. I want a full report. And I didn't get to finish my book about the knight!"

Cather laughed. "You're off on a grand adventure, my friend. You are my hero."

"I'm off on a quest with three people who hate me, no friends who have my back—and a very creepy woodsman to boot."

"That Count Monroe seems to like you."

"Yes, I'm glad he's going. But I'll miss you. Enough of my complaints—I don't even know how your visit with the queen went."

"Let me do your hair." Cather pulled out a chair and pushed her toward it. She quickly undid Mayten's braids and poured oil into her hands. The room smelled of coconuts as she gently rubbed the oil into Mayten's scalp, finger-combing the tangles. It felt like heaven, Mayten moaned in pleasure.

"I think I know what the issue is," Cather said as she worked. "But broaching the matter with the queen is a very delicate process."

"Why? What do you think is the problem?"

"There were two other children, a boy, and a girl, born between the prince and the twins. They died with the same sickness that took my sister—and your siblings." Cather paused for a moment, then took a deep breath. "That makes ten children she's given birth to. Part of the problem is that the queen is worn out from bearing so many children. But the loss of those two drained her as well."

Mayten wondered if her mother felt the same way. She'd never spoken of it. "Did she tell you all of that?"

"I . . . might have asked her maid a few questions."

"You're sneaky!" Mayten grinned, marveling at the transformation Cather was making to her hair. A braid started high on the right side of Mayten's head, wrapped around low on the left side, and draped down over her shoulder. The style made her look a bit older, she decided. A style that might be of help on the trip she was about to embark on.

Being that she was supposed to be leader, things might go easier if she looked the part.

Cather took a green ribbon and wove it expertly through the braid. "Servants are generally the ones who know the most about the people they serve. They also have the most at stake in keeping them well."

Mayten hadn't known anyone with servants before she'd come to the castle. How did Cather come up with these things?

"I hope I'll be able to find out more while you're gone. Perhaps she'll come to trust me. I'm fairly certain I know a few things that might help."

"Such as?" Mayten wished she had some of Cather's confidence. When it came to anything medicinal, Cather knew she was the expert.

"Well, first of all, I think it would help her to stop having babies."

Mayten laughed. "The king seems a very virile man."

"There are herbs a woman can take to keep pregnancies from happening."

Mayten gaped at her friend. "I never knew that."

Did her mother know about these herbs? If so, would she ever consider taking them?

She filed the information away in her mind for future reference. She'd had enough of babies for one lifetime. Nice to know there was an alternative.

A bell rang, calling them down to lunch. Mayten stood and examined her reflection in the mirror. She was happy to be back in her pants with a new shirt, a soft muslin fabric with billowing sleeves that had buttons on the wrists and laces up the neckline. The shirt had been added to her clothing pile along with a few other items.

Next to Cather, Mayten stood taller and thinner, her face longer and not so heart shaped. But her hair looked good in this braid, more like she felt. Older and perhaps a bit wiser.

Lunch went far too quickly in Mayten's estimation. Then the whole group, children included, headed outside to say goodbye. The questing team picked up their backpacks loaded with delicious food from the kitchen. Each pack had a thick sleeping quilt tied to it.

The children begged her to allow Anatolian to stay. Mayten shook her head just as Adven stepped forward. "No."

And that was that.

He likes my dog better than he likes me. The thought caught Mayten by surprise. She studied the group, wondering how she came to be in charge once again as she hugged each child and then Cather and Tray. The prince seemed full of nervous energy, shifting from one foot to another, too preoccupied to say a proper goodbye.

Finally, Adven gave the king a sharp nod and they were off.

The woodsman, Rafe, walked by Adven's side, in the position Hunter used to fill. An unexpected wave of grief washed over Mayten, and she blinked back tears. There should be no need for a woodsman on a trip this short. Why on earth were they taking one?

The prince followed close behind Adven, while Nan walked slightly in front of Mayten. Count Monroe brought up the rear, using his cane as a walking stick. Everyone was in their traveling clothes and sturdy boots.

The warm sun caressed her face, and for the first time in her life, Mayten felt reluctant to leave the open sky for the shadows of the thick forest. She had felt free in the castle, cut off from the distress of the trees. But ignoring their pain didn't make the pain go away. As soon as they left the trail across from the pond and stepped into the forest, the distress seeped back into her bones.

Anatolian seemed happy to be running through the oak woods again. He took off briskly down the trail, kicking dust into his recently washed fur. It was cooler in the trees, insects buzzed and birds chirped from the underbrush.

She took a couple of quick steps to catch up with Nan so they were walking side by side. "I had a chance to see your garden this morning."

Nan just kept walking.

After hearing how Cather had used the maid to gather information, Mayten had decided to do her own investigating. Each person on this team had a specific bit of information, information that could help her understand what was happening with the trees.

Nan was a botanist and had done the most research.

Count Monroe was a respected historian and probably knew the most about the forest in the broader sense.

The prince had grown up with the trees and rode his horse through the woods. It was quite possible he had something to offer.

Even the woodsman, Rafe, knew things about this forest—if she could work up the nerve to approach him.

She had to start by earning their trust.

"I was quite impressed," Mayten continued. She was determined to get this girl to talk.

Nan gave her a sideways glance, clamped her lips shut, and turned away.

How would Cather deal with this situation? Mayten thought a moment and pressed on. "My da is a famous gardener in our area. He would be amazed at what you've done."

A smile played at the corners of Nan's lips. "Really?" she said without looking at Mayten. "Do you by chance know what he uses for fertilizer? I have developed a rotating system of taking all the table scraps from the kitchen and mixing them with horse manure. It is a process of decomposition I've perfected over the years, and I believe I have the formulations about right, but am always looking to improve."

"I'm not sure." Mayten kept her own smile hidden. She hadn't expected the princess to respond so quickly. "I think he just sings to them."

Nan turned and stared at her in disbelief. "*Sings* to them?"

She sniffed, turned on her heel, and stalked after the others.

Puzzled, Mayten caught up with the princess. "What do you have against singers?"

The girl glared at her.

"I'm a *scientist*," she said as though speaking to a child. "What you are describing is nothing but witchcraft."

She hurried to catch up with her brother, leaving Mayten standing alone, feeling like she'd just been slapped.

CHAPTER TWENTY-SIX

Count Monroe caught up with Mayten. "My dear, are you well? You look a bit flustered."

She glanced down in surprise as her hand brushed Anatolian's back. Last time she'd seen him, he'd been chasing down a scent. Had he sensed her distress?

Mayten forced her feet to move, stroking the dog's soft fur as the smell of oranges drifted over her, calming her ruffled nerves. "You might not understand this, but all my life I've thought everyone loved singers. Trained singers are held in high esteem in our clan . . ."

One glance at the count's kind face and words tumbled out. "Then I learned that Adven hates singers, though I don't know why. This morning the king told me a story about an evil singer who sucked energy from trees and even killed a dog! His grandfather *banned* singers from the castle. Now Nan tells me she thinks singers use witchcraft. Witchcraft!"

She stopped and faced the count. "Has the world gone mad?"

Her face flushed with heat, realizing she'd poured out her grief to a man she didn't really know.

"Witchcraft?" the count muttered. "That *is* absurd."

Count Monroe's soft assurance calmed her and they walked on.

"Singers have a history of aligning with nature to help things grow," he said. "They aren't using outside forces, just encouraging the life force already present within."

"Tell that to the princess." Anger grew inside as Mayten remembered Nan's disdain. The trail was winding up a hill and she dug her feet into the earth with a vengeance.

The count started wheezing and finally stopped. "I'm sorry. My lungs are not what they used to be. I'm afraid I have to move a bit slower."

"No, I'm the one who should be sorry." She was supposed to be leading this group, not having a childish temper tantrum. "Please forgive my rant."

She waited for him to catch his breath, then started at a slower pace. "How do you know so much about singing—if you don't mind my asking?"

"A historian is a lifelong student of all things. I have interviewed countless singers, healers, travelers, crafters—you name it. I could—and have—written volumes on each subject."

Mayten's heart skipped a beat. "Do you know about the evil singer then? The one the king told me about? I've never heard about him."

"Oh yes, he is a particular interest of mine. And I wouldn't call him 'evil.' Most people, once you get to know them, have reasons for what they do."

"Did you know him?" she asked. "Personally?"

He laughed. "No dear, I'm not *that* old."

Once again, heat flushed her face. She glanced away, embarrassed, but he didn't seem at all insulted. "But he took energy from plants and killed a dog! That goes against everything a singer is taught."

"True, but think for a moment. Be honest now, Mayten. Have you never thought about taking energy for yourself? Most of the singers I've interviewed have at least thought about it."

She fell silent. Of course, she'd thought about it. The temptation hid, like a dirty little secret, tempting her when she was tired. How easy it would be to take a sip of tree energy . . .

She would never actually do it, though. No singer would.

At least, that's what she'd thought before hearing the king's story.

Could the count be right? Did all singers consider the temptation?

What about Mother? When she was exhausted from caring for so many children along with her clan responsibilities did *she* ever think about it?

Had she ever tried?

It didn't seem out of the realm of possibility, a realization that disturbed Mayten beyond thought.

She firmly shook the idea from her head. "I'd never do such a thing and neither would my mother."

"That's good," the count said with a nod. "You and your Mother are noble indeed."

Mayten didn't know if she was noble, but she could tell right from wrong and loved the idea she might be like her mother— at least in character.

They walked in silence as the hill crested. The trail led down a gentle slope into a canyon filled with redwoods. Mayten's favorite trees. How could anyone hurt something so majestic?

Anatolian kept pressed close to her side as they walked, calming her. He'd always been in tune with her feelings. She was grateful her mother had sent him on this quest. His presence had been a constant comfort to her.

"Have you given any thought as to why the trees are dying? Have you seen anything like this blight in your travels?" She kept her gaze on the trail, not sure she wanted to see the count's expression. Light filtered through the trees, leaving dappled shadows on the ground as the forest thickened. Soft duff covered the ground, quieting their footsteps.

"I did come across a similar situation when I was in Caspia. That's one reason I wanted to come along on this expedition, to see if it might be the same thing. We had quite a mystery on our hands there too. Turned out to be a bug so small it was invisible to the naked eye. The infestation decimated thousands of trees."

Fear crawled up Mayten's arms like thousands of angry ants. "If that's true, then more than this forest is in trouble. The king sent shiploads of logs from affected trees to other ports."

The count nodded. "So I heard. I was quite worried last night but didn't want to cause undue alarm. Not until we had more information."

"Stopping here," yelled Adven, who had walked down into the canyon of old-growth redwood trees.

Why were they stopping so early? Mayten wondered. Adven usually drove them until they were exhausted. Was he being careful because the prince and the princess were along?

Or perhaps he'd noticed the count was having difficulty keeping up.

When she and Monroe arrived at the camp, Adven and the others were gathering firewood. Adven dropped a load of branches on the ground as they stepped into the clearing.

Count Monroe dropped his pack onto the ground, wheezing. Should she have offered to carry it for the older man? He did not look well.

Adven waved an arm at the trees. "Go do—whatever it is you do. That's why we're here, after all. But stay within shouting distance."

Mayten waited, expecting to feel the sting of wounded pride. But Adven was right. That was her reason for being here.

She went off the trail into the woods, Anatolian by her side. The peace of the old-growth redwoods surrounded her as the duff beneath her feet thickened. The trees were giants. She craned her neck to try and see their tops but it was impossible. As she passed each one, she reached out to touch their soft furry bark and say hello. Rich green ferns contrasted with the rust red of the tree bark.

Anatolian darted in front of her and growled. Mayten froze as a man rounded a tree a few paces ahead. Rafe, the woodsman, slowed and kept his distance from the dog, glaring at her as he went by. He was a thin man with ropey muscles. He wore a large hunting knife on his belt on one side and a hatchet on the other. The look in his eyes said he'd rather kill her than talk to her.

"What's his problem?" she whispered to Anatolian when the man was out of earshot. She stroked Anatolian's head, grateful for the millionth time to have him by her side.

Rafe hadn't been carrying an armload of wood and he hadn't brought back a rabbit or other game. What on earth was he up to?

She let herself relax, reaching for that ancient connection with the gentle giants around her. Some of these trees had been around for centuries. Most were so wide she couldn't get her arms around an eighth of their trunks and there were no low branches to swing up on.

Of course, she didn't need to climb in order to listen, but she liked to be as close to a tree as possible.

She scouted around and found a burned-out hollow similar to the hollow she'd fallen asleep in following Hunter's devastating encounter with the mountain lion. This tree dwarfed that tree, though. The hollow could have held a small family.

And she had it all to herself—almost. Mayten crawled into the hollow and Anatolian followed. Had the early island people once lived in here? The tree certainly seemed old enough.

She ran her hand over the smooth burn as her eyes adjusted to the shadowed interior. The only smell was that of damp soil. These trees were survivors, adapting to the harshest conditions, even fire.

She could learn something from that. They all could learn from the trees.

:Hello, Grandfather.:

:Hello, child.:

Surprised at the prompt response, Mayten said the first words that came to mind. :What pains you, Grandfather?:

Stupid, she snapped to herself. She should have asked a more specific question. This giant tree, unlike those trees that lived in more exposed areas, had shallow roots. That's why the redwoods preferred canyons out of the wind. Their roots intertwined with other trees, keeping them standing for eons. The groves stood together as a family stood together.

This particular tree had likely been standing for several thousand years and was connected, in consciousness, through its root system, to hundreds of other trees.

Pictures, feelings, and impressions from the tree's extensive history flooded her: strife among people the trees had loved, animals that had scarred their bark, beetle infestations, droughts, the birth of a fawn, a nest of hatching eggs . . . the memories took Mayten on emotional highs then crashed back to earth, reliving the devastating events of history.

Clan wars between the first inhabitants of the island.

The struggle for existence when outlanders came.

Memories a thousand years old, including the terrifying fire over five hundred years ago, flooded her mind and heart. The images kept pounding at her, over and over, until she could take no more . . .

The sound of Anatolian barking dragged her free of the tree's memories. She was curled up like a newborn on the floor of the hollowed-out space, her face wet with tears. She crawled from the tree, touching the wood gently and sending what peace she could.

Someone stood in front of the tree, hand stretched out to help her. It was the prince.

"Are you okay?" he said, his voice full of concern.

She took his hand, looking about in confusion. "Why is it so dark?"

"You've been gone for hours. Adven got worried." He led the way back to camp, keeping hold of her hand. She didn't pull away, still shaken from experiencing the memories of thousands of years of pain and joy. Her feet felt like lead, stumbling and tripping over the smallest bump.

When they got to the edge of camp, he dropped her hand.

"Adven's worried?" she asked, startled by the sudden feeling of loss. She missed the warmth of his hand, the connection with another human.

"I think so. He's grumbling a lot, and he sent me to look for you. We ate dinner hours ago. We're about ready to turn in for the night."

"Really?" Mayten didn't know what was more startling, that she'd lost so much time, or that Adven had worried about her.

CHAPTER TWENTY-SEVEN

The sun was just lighting the canyon of the redwoods where the team had camped. The air had a crisp feel and smelled of pine. Most everyone was still rolled in their blankets when Mayten stretched and scrambled to her feet. Adven already had a fire going and water boiling.

"What do you need to do today?" Adven looked impatient, as usual. He wasn't used to waiting on others to make decisions.

"Do?" she said, holding her hands toward the fire.

"This is your show, Singer." Adven poked at the coals violently enough to send sparks crackling into the air. "Do we stay here? Do we go on? What?"

Mayten wasn't sure. She didn't want to talk with the grandfather tree again, she knew that. She had thousands of years of memories to sift through. She needed to find a younger tree to talk to, one with a shorter memory. "Let's move on. Don't have to go too far, another couple of hours in?"

Adven nodded and pulled out the cook pot. He refused to look at her as he pulled a package—wrapped in cloth and tied with string—from his pack. Her mouth watered as she watched him slice several pieces of bacon into the pot. The bacon sizzled as soon as it hit the hot metal, surrounding them in the enticing smell that could only belong to frying pork.

In no time, the rest of the team was gathered around the fire. No one said much, more focused on downing coffee and scarfing bacon than conversation.

The others packed while Adven cleaned up. Mayten had eaten twice as much as usual and still felt as though she needed more sleep. She took the rear position when they moved out. She had to come up with some sort of plan.

The trail wound back out of the canyon on the far side and the redwood trees were replaced with oaks and thinner lodge-pole pine. The air cooled as they climbed and a herd of deer fled as they hiked, recalling the nightmarish memories of Hunter's encounter with the mountain lion.

Mayten stopped to pull on a sweater, grateful to whoever had thought to include it in her supplies. To her astonishment, the prince dropped back to walk with her. He seemed happier since they'd left the castle, his face smooth instead of lined with worry.

"Are you okay?" he asked as he approached. "You looked pretty shook-up last night. Did the tree . . . tell you . . . say something? Sorry, I'm not sure how it works. Did you hear something—unsettling?"

She laughed at his hesitation. He seemed almost . . . human. Perhaps now was a good time to find out what he might know about singers and the trees. She tightened the straps on her pack as they continued up the trail.

"What's so funny?" he asked, his eyes narrowing as if he was trying to decide whether or not he should be mad.

"You seem . . . happy, is all. I think questing agrees with you."

Anatolian dashed by after a squirrel.

He smiled shyly at first, as if embarrassed, then broadly, with a smile that lit up his face. "I've wanted to go on a quest since I was nine, but Father wouldn't let me. 'The king gets what the king wants,'" he said in a singsong voice.

She laughed again. "I actually heard him say something like that."

"What was he trying to get out of you?" He looked at her with sudden interest.

"He wants me to come back in two years, after my training, and bring an initiate. Then take one or two of your siblings and train them as singers."

He laughed. It was the first time she'd heard him laugh, and the sound echoed off the walls of the hillside next to them. Adven glanced back from the front of the line, then turned to continue on. The prince's laugh was surprisingly melodious, like water running over rocks in a brook. "I can promise you—changing his mind when he's set on something is like trying to move a granite slab the size of a horse. It took me ten years to wear him down about the quest. Would you like to come back?"

He looked strangely hopeful and Mayten's stomach gave a little quiver, like she'd swallowed butterflies.

Probably just lonely, she told herself. He had no brothers close to his age at the castle and his older sisters seemed focused on their own interests.

"I don't know," she answered truthfully. "Before this quest, I never wanted anything but my own clan and eventually my own homestead. Now that I've seen more of the world, I realize . . . there is just so *much* to see."

She glanced at the beautiful clouds in the azure sky visible above them. This view was majestic and she would never had seen it if she hadn't come.

The quest had opened her eyes to a whole new world. Not only had she lost a friend, the first time she'd experienced the death of someone close to her age, she'd met a king and visited his castle and gardens. And she was learning what it meant to be a leader.

Could she go back to her old life, training under her mother, caring for her brothers and sisters? It all seemed so . . . small. The idea of staying at home felt like wearing a shirt she'd outgrown, tight and uncomfortable.

"That's how I feel," the prince said. "I've been with Father on a few of his diplomatic visits. I've seen a little of the world and I want to see more. The castle feels confining to me."

Good thing they weren't headed to her clan. If he thought the castle was confining, a clan her size would likely make him feel like he'd been stuck in a cellar.

"You never answered my question," he said. "Did the tree tell you anything? Does listening sap your energy in some way?"'

She thought a moment. "Do you have relatives that like to hear themselves talk? And you kind of avoid them because you know that once they have your attention, they won't stop talking about their aches and pains and telling 'Back in my day . . .' stories?"

He laughed. "The man who runs our livery is like that. Every time I go out to get my horse, I feel like I'm slinking around trying to avoid him."

"This tree was kind of like that. I asked one question and got a two-thousand-year history of pain, joy, and agony. Having all that dumped on me at once was exhausting."

"That's amazing. I didn't realize trees could talk like that."

"They don't really use physical voices. It's more like sharing visual images."

"I guess I'd like to *see* that then. Two thousand years! No wonder you looked so . . ."

She felt her cheeks warm. "How bad was it?"

She had little memory of anything beyond the warmth of the prince's hand as he guided her back to the camp.

"You looked like, you know, you were sick or something. Pale and weak. Everyone was worried. Count Monroe sat next to you patting your hand half the night."

"He did?" She'd have to thank the old man. She saw him up ahead, enjoying the view as he walked. She'd been so lost in her thoughts she hadn't considered how the others must've felt when she'd been gone so long. Now that she thought back on it, Adven hadn't even yelled at her. She *must* have looked pretty bad.

Heat flushed her cheeks again and a lump rose in her throat. She was either going to die of embarrassment or burst into tears if they didn't start talking about something else. "Prince Thomas, do you have any ideas about why the trees are dying?"

"Please, call me Tom." The prince—Tom—walked in silence for so long she thought he might have forgotten her question. He glanced around as they walked, his brow furrowed in concentration.

"Not about the trees," he finally said. "But I've noticed changes in the forest itself when Sterling and I go out for a ride."

"Sterling?" She didn't remember meeting anyone by that name at the castle.

"My horse."

Mayten nodded. She chewed her lip a moment, but before she could ask the prince to elaborate, he continued.

"I've come across more dead animals lately. At first it was only small creatures—chipmunks and squirrels. One day I found a deer beside the trail. There were no marks on any of the dead animals, except the deer had a broken leg. I guess it could have starved to death. But it didn't look that skinny."

Mayten shivered. She remembered the dog that had been killed by the evil singer and her stomach churned.

"It made me wonder if their deaths could have been caused by the same thing that was attacking the trees," the prince said. "I know that probably sounds crazy. But maybe they ate something that grew on the trees and were poisoned?"

Mayten shrugged and the prince frowned. "Then I saw a dead bear. There wasn't a mark on him that I could see. Bears don't eat anything that grows on trees around here. They eat berries mostly—and fish, I guess. I got the heebie-jeebies seeing the bear like that."

"Heebie-jeebies?" she asked, but her mind had already begun to draw conclusions.

"Like when you think you see a ghost."

Mayten nodded absently. She glanced up and saw the count walking beside Nan close behind Adven and Rafe. Was he telling her about what he'd seen in Caspia?

She waved a hand at the pair. "I think I need to talk to your sister."

"No problem," he called after her as she jogged away.

It didn't take long to catch up. She slowed to a walk beside Nan, trying to steady her breathing. "Princess, do you mind if I ask you a question?"

Nan looked at her from the corner of her eye, not taking her focus off the trail. The count gave Mayten a nod and dropped back a few paces.

"Count Monroe said when he was in Caspia, they had a similar issue with the trees. He said it turned out to be an infestation of tiny bugs—too small to see with your eyes—that killed thousands of trees."

"Infestation?" Nan said, her lips turning up on one side as if she'd tasted something bad.

"Yes. He said they'd lost thousands of trees, which frankly has us both worried that the trees your father sent to all the ports could spread the sickness."

The princess stopped abruptly and planted her fists on her hips. "Do you actually think I'd be that stupid? Any infestation strong enough to kill trees would leave marks, scars, trails, something. I told you these trees had no sign of that."

"Okaaaay." Mayten stared at the other girl, blinking in surprise at the princess's reaction. Nan glared at her, eyebrows furrowed in anger. The count caught up with them.

"My ears were burning," he said with a smile. "Were you lovely ladies talking about me?"

"Yes," Mayten said. "I was just telling the princess what you shared with me about the trees in Caspia."

"Oh my, yes. That was quite a devastating time."

Nan gave them a grumpy-teacher-with-slow-students look. "Invisible or not, infestations leave traces on the wood of a tree. The wood tells us—"

"We'll stop here," Adven yelled.

"There's a small lake about twenty minutes from here if I remember correctly," the count called. "It would be nice to rest by the lake."

To Mayten's surprise, Adven looked at Rafe. The woodsman nodded and Adven continued up the trail.

Nan extended her lecture all the way to the lake. The count seemed fascinated, asking question after question about wood mites and beetles. Mayten's mind wandered to the memories the ancient tree had given her. She sorted through them as best she could, trying to make sense of them all.

Her first sight of the lake took her breath away. The water was a clear emerald blue. Soft sandy banks and shimmering aspen trees lined the shore.

The woodlands had been changing ever since they left the canyon. Now they were surrounded by an alpine forest with fir and pine trees scenting the air with their tang. Mayten could almost taste the pine sap on her tongue. They must have climbed a thousand feet to find a forest like this one. She shivered and stopped to pull her jacket from her pack.

Had Mother ever traveled this far? She was certain her mother would love to see this. Thinking of Mother brought another image to mind—Mother's little book. Mayten was anxious to talk to these new trees. She felt as though an answer was close at hand—

"Mayten," Tom called to her. He and the count stood on the shoreline a few paces from the lake's gently lapping waves. "Does Anatolian like the water? Is it okay if he goes in?"

"He loves it, and yes!" Anatolian would chase a stick into water for hours. It was one of his favorite things to do. He would be ecstatic to have someone play with him for a while.

The count handed the prince a small branch and he threw it. Anatolian bounded into the water before the stick splashed down, surging toward the floating wood with powerful strokes.

That would keep the prince and the count busy. Mayten picked up her pack, her jaw set in determination. She had some reading to do.

CHAPTER TWENTY-EIGHT

A s Adven and Nan set up the camp, Rafe went off to hunt. Mayten found a pine tree at the edge of the lake that was far enough from the others that she wouldn't be disturbed yet close enough to watch Anatolian splash into the water as the prince threw the stick over and over. Count Monroe laughed and clapped, a happy audience of one.

Mayten inhaled the fresh pine scent and let her fingers play with the dirt and pine needles all around her. The little book lay in her lap, open to Level One: *Cometh to the tree with humility and silence.*

She'd practiced this level over and over until it became second nature.

She turned to Level Two: *Putteth away childish concerns and press more deeply into listening with all of your senses.*

In other words, learn everything you could about trees— taste, touch, smell—in order to listen in a deeper way. She'd incorporated this practice into her life on a daily basis as well.

She flipped to Level Three: *You must confideth in the trees and grow to love them as trusted friends.*

During this level, talking to the trees became normal. She loved this level. The trees were like her extended family and talking to them was natural.

She turned to Level Four: *You must open your mind and heart to receiveth images from the tree celebrating your likeness and communion with the trees. These communications are pure gift.*

This level was more mystical than the previous levels. She'd had trouble . . .

With a flash of pride, Mayten realized she'd been receiving messages from the trees without really trying. She thought about the tree that had comforted her after Hunter's accident by sending peaceful images. The tree's message had indeed felt like a gift.

. . . which brought her to Level Five: *You must go deeper. Communeth with the trees, their roots, their animal messengers, and their relatives.*

She had also experienced that level. She understood the trees' connection to the greater island and possibly beyond.

She continued on through the book.

Level Six includes your ability to sendeth messages across this community of living things to others through your tree family. This is only possible with great trust and love.

She had managed to receive messages from her mother through the trees and had, hopefully, sent messages back.

Level Seven, when your heart is ready, when there is great love and trust, you may have an experience of unification in which you will lose yourself and blendeth into all things, becoming one with all.

She had not experienced Level Seven, the final level. Not yet. But she could easily send visual images to the tree and receive them. She didn't understand what was meant by 'unity with the trees.' Her mother said many singers never got to that final stage.

". . . *have an experience of unification in which you will lose yourself and blendeth into all things* . . ."

Whatever did that mean?

No matter. She was certain she had what she needed to discover what was hurting the trees. It was what came after she wasn't sure about.

Finally, Mayten reached the section she wanted to reread. This section went into detail about the benefits and abuses of exchanging energy with the trees. The more she read, the more certain she became—someone was stealing energy from the trees.

That was why the trees had sent her a picture of a man from two hundred years ago.

There was another evil singer around.

Count Monroe had seemed sure that stealing energy was a common temptation for singers. Nan had said that infestations would leave traces behind.

There was no trace of anything wrong in the dead trees. Or in the dead animals.

Which led to one conclusion—someone had taken their life energy.

Mayten shuddered. She set the book in her lap and rubbed her arms, feeling a chill run through her. She turned to face the tree and pressed her hands to the bark. Perhaps her mother had sent another message.

The world fell away until she was completely focused on the tree and heard . . . nothing.

Frustrated, she tried again, forcing her body to relax, breathing so that her mind could listen better. A memory popped into her mind, completely unrelated to her current situation. Her family stood in a circle with their bare feet touching the ground during thanks-giving. It wasn't a new memory, there were no pregnant sisters or brothers-in-law in the circle, just her small family.

Why would her mother send her this memory? Was she, once again, reminding Mayten that she was loved and missed?

Mayten sighed. Although she enjoyed the memory, she'd been hoping for something more practical, something that could help her figure out what to do.

She stood and brushed dirt and needles from her pants. There was one more person left to talk to—the woodsman. He seemed skittish around her, ducking away whenever she came near. She'd thought perhaps he held the same aversion toward singers as Adven did. Was it possible the woodsman was the evil singer?

Fear tingled up her spine. She clenched her jaws and refused to panic. If that was the case, she had others around. She would tell Adven and he'd . . .

He'd what? Adven hated her.

The prince then, and the count—

A commotion from camp caught her attention. The prince, Count Monroe, and Anatolian were all watching two figures Mayten could not identify. Someone appeared to be hurt, leaning heavily on Adven who was struggling with the other's weight.

Rafe, Mayten realized with a jolt. It was the woodsman.

She raced toward the camp, urging her legs to move faster.

When she reached the others, the woodsman was stretched out on the ground, a blanket covering him and a rolled blanket under his head.

Pain washed over Mayten followed rapidly by sorrow. The scene was too much like one she'd experienced not that long ago.

Adven and Nan leaned over the woodsman while the others hovered nearby. Anatolian ran to her side, shaking water from his coat and whining anxiously.

She held the dog away from the woodsman. "What happened?"

Adven looked at her, panic in his one good eye. He felt the same way she did.

The shock sent Mayten back a step. Then she squared her shoulders and met Adven's eyes.

"Someone's been trapping here," Adven said with a look of disgust. "One of those imported metal traps. It got his leg. It was almost impossible to get the thing off."

Mayten's stomach lurched. She hated blood. Her stomach felt queasy even thinking about it. She studied Rafe's pain-twisted face.

How long would it take to run back down to the castle and bring back a healer? The thought was followed quickly by another—what if he *was* the evil singer?

Then she remembered her conversation with Cather, how similar their experiences with energy had seemed.

Could Mayten heal him?

She'd never thought of such a thing before. In her clan, roles were clearly defined. In an emergency, however, it would be okay to try, wouldn't it?

Another look at Rafe's clenched eyes, at the pain contorting his face, convinced her. She had to try. No matter who he was, he didn't deserve to suffer. Not if she could help.

She kneeled next to the woodsman.

"What are you doing?" Adven demanded.

Mayten hunched her shoulders at the fear and anger in Adven's voice. Would he try to pull her away? Strike her?

She placed her hands on Rafe's chest as she'd seen Cather do so many times before. His eyes rolled and he started to thrash. Adven moved to his shoulders and held him down. He gave her a quick nod when she glanced at him in surprise.

"Prince Thomas, hold his legs," she directed.

Thomas moved in and grabbed Rafe's legs without questioning her command. The woodsman shrieked in pain but Tom held on.

"I've never done this before, but I *have* to try to help him. Please hold him still and don't ask questions. I need to focus."

Mayten blocked out the noise and commotion around her. She searched for his energy as though he were a tree. It was not hard to find, yet felt completely different from tree energy. The woodsman's energy was warm, pulsing, rich, almost . . . tasty—

Revulsion roiled through her, tightening her gut so she almost vomited. She kept a gentle connection with his energy and refocused on Rafe's physical body.

Starting at his head, she traced the flow of energy down. Again she felt the pulse, regular and . . . when she reached his injured leg, the energy amplified, becoming loud and angry, hurting Mayten's ears.

Cather had explained how she sent her own energy into the wound.

Mayten breathed deeply and pictured energy flowing through her hands, down into the man's leg. She began to hum, sending her vocal vibrations through her hands along his spine to his leg.

Rafe stopped squirming and became still. He began to breathe more evenly.

When Mayten again reached the injury, there was so much noise, so much confusion . . . she wasn't sure what to do next. She lifted her hands, sat back on her heels and thought.

"Well?" Adven kept his hands on Rafe's shoulders. "Why did you stop?"

She raised a hand. "Give me a moment."

She placed her hands on Rafe's chest and tried to visualize the leg like the branch of a tree. As she sent the energy down the branch, she found the branch twisted, broken.

"Let me see his foot." She nodded at the prince. Tom lifted the bottom of the blanket.

Rafe's boot was bent at a strange angle.

"We have to straighten his leg," she said to Adven. "Sorry Rafe, this is going to hurt."

She turned to the prince. "Tom, trade places with Adven. Hold down his shoulders."

According to Tray, setting bones was part of a traveler's training. Adven knew how to handle this type of injury—she hoped.

Mayten sat back on her heels while Adven moved into place. Without warning, he yanked on Rafe's leg. The woodsman screamed and the forest fell silent. He bucked and tried to sit up, but Tom held him tight to the ground.

A quick glance at Nan showed her face so white Mayten was afraid she would faint. The count stepped up to take Nan's arm, but he didn't look much better.

Mayten took a deep breath and laid her hands on Rafe again. He relaxed as soon as she touched him.

Quickly, she followed the energy down. Now she could see clearly where the branch was broken. She sent her energy to the break, using all her will to knit the bone together.

The energy chaos surrounding the leg quieted. Her energy flowed through him—soothing the bone, the muscles, the skin—leaving calm, peace, relief.

And then blackness overtook her.

CHAPTER TWENTY-NINE

Someone was playing a flute . . . and . . . was that Taiwania singing?

Confused and disoriented, Mayten struggled to open her eyes. Had she died and her spirit somehow returned to home?

The idea did not frighten her. In fact, it gave her a measure of joy and peace.

Home.

Wood smoke stung her nose, the scent of burning fir shattering the illusion of being home. Da only burned pine at home. Fir burned too fast, too hot.

Mayten forced her eyes open. Stars twinkled high overhead, and firelight flickered over fir boughs—

"She's awake!" Count Monroe gave her a smile that lit his face. He sat awkwardly on his pack beside her, hands atop his knees.

She was still a bit groggy. The count rose to his feet and helped her sit up.

Anatolian licked her cheek. Nan and Tom sat up straighter and smiled at her. Adven sat on his haunches, sipping from a cup, watching her.

"Are you okay?" asked Nan and Tom at the same time.

She nodded. Their concern touched her. Adven shoved a plate of food at her. At first, Mayten didn't think she could eat. Then the aroma of bacon reached her and she realized she was famished.

The image of Tray shoving cheese in his mouth made her slow down, shocked she'd consumed almost half the food on her plate. She glanced around, trying to get her bearings.

A figure lay on the far side of the fire, still and unmoving. Rafe.

"Is he dead?" Mayten asked, fear hammering in her chest. "Did I kill him?"

Adven laughed, a gravelly sound she'd last heard during one of Hunter's campfire stories. He took her plate, refilled it, and handed it back. "Sleeping. As impossible as it might sound, I think you healed him."

Her eyes filled with tears which she hurriedly blinked away. Losing two woodsmen would have been hard on Adven. And losing the king's best woodsman . . . who knew what that would mean.

She stared down at her plate, no longer hungry. "I've never done anything like that before."

"I've never *seen* anything like it." Nan stepped up to the fire and warmed her hands. "There's no scientific explanation."

"It's not supernatural," the count said. "Not in the way you're thinking, Princess. What Mayten did concerns the flow of energy."

Nan chewed her bottom lip, apparently lost in thought.

"I can't believe I've never thought of it myself," the count muttered. "A tree singer who can heal. It makes perfect sense. Mayten gave her energy to Rafe as she repaired the damage in his leg. That's why she's so tired . . . and hungry." He turned to her. "Am I right?"

Mayten nodded. "It's the way we work with trees. Only we don't get drained by it. That was the most exhausting thing I've ever done. How long did I sleep?"

"You were out for four hours," the prince said. "I—we—were very worried."

"I thought maybe you gave too much," the count said. He stared at her as if mystified. "Healers learn to give only a certain amount of their life force but you are untrained. You could have killed yourself."

"But how did I get over here?" Mayten asked. Her last memory was kneeling over the woodsman.

"I . . . ," the prince started, then turned bright red. "We carried you here after you fainted."

Mayten stared at him a moment, struggling to understand what was going on. Nan gave her brother a light punch in the shoulder.

Mayten decided to change the subject. "When I woke up, there was the most beautiful singing. I thought maybe I'd died."

"That was Nan," Tom said as the princess glanced away. "She has the best voice in the castle."

A scientist who could sing. Looked like Princess Nan was more than just a grumpy gardener.

Mayten set her plate aside and lay back down on her blanket. "I'd love to hear more—if you don't mind."

The princess seemed to shrink into herself, clearly uncomfortable with praise. She leaned over and whispered in the prince's ear. He picked up a flute and began to play as Nan sang of love and loss and a pain so deep Mayten wondered if Nan had experienced such a love story herself. As she sang, the firelight transformed her face into that of an angel.

Mayten pulled the blanket snug around her shoulders. Funny how faces could be transformed.

A simple smile had transformed the prince's face, turning it from an angry boy into a handsome young man.

Pain had transformed Rafe's face into a mask of agony.

Even Count Monroe's face had transformed during their journey. When he'd clapped with delight over Anatolian's antics, the count looked as though years had fallen away.

ℬ

Mayten slept deeply, waking to the cheerful sounds of Anatolian splashing in the lake and the smell of frying onions. She sat up, rubbing sleep from her eyes. The sun was already up. Adven squatted by the fire, poking at whatever he'd stuck in the cooking pan. He forked potatoes onto two plates, stalked over and handed her one of the plates.

Rafe watched groggily from the opposite side of the fire. He was sitting up but looked pale and disoriented. No one else was around.

"Where is everyone?" Mayten asked as she took the plate.

Adven walked around the fire to Rafe and handed the woodsman the second plate. "Monroe is off taking notes on I don't know what, the botanist is off kissing plants, and I'm here babysitting invalids."

His eyes glinted with what might have been a touch of mischief.

Mayten nibbled at a potato, letting the salty taste fill her mouth. Odd how she didn't take offense at the 'invalid' remark. That was just the way he talked, as much a part of him as the gravelly voice.

"What happened?" Rafe asked. He pulled up his pant leg and examined the wound. No blood, no scab, only healing skin with a crescent of pink scars. "It's tender but . . ."

"You can thank that one." Adven waved his coffee mug at Mayten.

"What?" Rafe seemed at a loss for words.

"What do you remember?" Adven asked. He looked genuinely interested.

"I remember stepping on that damn trap. Those things have been outlawed in the kingdom since they were invented. 'Tis not an honest way to hunt. I remember screaming bloody murder for help. I remember you coming to get that thing off me. I think I must've passed out then. The only thing I remember after that was you slapping my face and helping me stumble back to camp."

"I couldn't very well carry you," Adven said. "You may look like a twig but you're heavy as an ox."

The woodsman shrugged. "Mostly, I remember the pain. Like someone snapped my leg clean in two."

"Your leg was broken, all right. I'm afraid I didn't help things trying to get you out of that trap."

"Not sure if I can put weight on it yet." Rafe winced as he stretched the leg flat on the ground.

"You should have Cather look at it when we get back or one of the king's healers," Mayten said. "I'm not certain I put it all right."

"I remember when you put your hands on me." Rafe stared at the fire, plate forgotten in his hands. "I was so afraid you were a witch, that your hands would burn me out of existence. But as soon as you touched me, this . . . peace flowed all the way from my head ta my leg. I ain't felt nothin' like it." He took a deep breath. His haughty expression was gone, as was his scowl. "Then the pain went down and I could breathe again."

He carefully set his plate to one side, then looked directly at her. "I was raised ta fear singers. Heard lots of stories growing up. Almost like ghost stories. That's why I come, ta keep an eye on the king's children, keep 'em safe from ya. But I'll not believe them stories now. Never again will I let someone speak ill of ya. I'm thankful, Singer. I would've lost my leg and my living if it weren't for you."

Mayten felt a flush creep up her neck. She didn't know what to say.

"Don't get a big head," Adven said. "You've proven your worth as a healer. We're still waiting for you to prove yourself as a singer."

He turned away and began to clean the cook pot. Mayten watched in disbelief. Had she read the man wrong? He'd seemed almost to *like* her when she'd first woken.

Perhaps she'd been dreaming—

"What do we do today? Stay or move on?" Adven asked.

The change of subject left her reeling.

"We'll stay here," she said with as much authority as she could muster. "I need more time with the trees."

Adven was right. She hadn't proven herself a true singer. Not yet.

CHAPTER THIRTY

Mayten took her time finding the right tree. She walked among the birches, away from the lake. To her dismay, several of the trees she tried to listen to were already dead. The trees stood tall just like their companions, but no matter how hard she listened, they had no voice. She'd left Anatolian with the prince at the lake and could hear his happy barking. His joy was a stark contrast to the emptiness she felt from the trees.

The first and only time she'd accidentally taken too much energy from a plant she'd felt it die. Cold, empty, alone.

Just like these trees.

Death's darkness washed over her as she moved from tree to tree. Mayten shivered, feeling as though winter held her in its icy grasp. Someone was indeed draining life from the trees. Someone who'd been here recently.

Should they go back and tell the king? He had said they were only gathering information. Or should she keep looking, hoping to stumble upon whoever was draining the trees? That seemed as likely as finding a teardrop in the ocean.

Her mother's book had been crystal clear on one point: taking the life of living things was the only offense among tree singers that warranted death.

If she did find the person responsible, they had to die for their crimes.

Mayten glanced around, half expecting to see a dark figure materialize in the trees ahead.

She needed more time. Time to think, to organize her thoughts.

But first, she needed to find a living tree.

She wandered deeper into the forest, touching trees—fat trees, skinny trees, trees gnarled from disease. To her great relief, many of these trees still sang with life energy. She needed one at least two hundred years old, old enough to have memories of the last time trees had died in this manner, but not so old she'd be overwhelmed by too many memories.

Finally, she found a white pine tree—alive and willing to talk. She made herself comfortable on the ground by its trunk. A pang squeezed her heart when she reached out to put a hand on Anatolian's head. She so missed having him by her side.

He's having fun at the lake, she reminded herself.

She closed her eyes and began. :*Hello, Auntie.*:

:*Hello, Daughter.*: Of course, the tree did not speak in words. Their communication flowed in pictures, images of shade, branches sheltering from the rain. With a start, Mayten realized she had no trouble understanding these images.

She wasn't quite sure how to begin. :*I need help.*:

:*Anything, child, within my ability to offer.*:

:*Can you tell me who or what is hurting the trees?*:

The tree sent more images—the face of a man, dying trees, the upsetting of the seasons—confirming what she'd come to suspect.

Someone was murdering trees again. Just like the evil singer had done two hundred years ago. He . . . or she . . . was out here somewhere.

Again, the face appeared before her. She tried to explain that too much time had passed. The man could no longer be alive.

Insistent, the face swam in her mind, taunting her with a vague sense of familiarity. The man had been handsome with black curls, tall and thin. His eyes were haughty in the manner of one who thinks others beneath him. His skin was unlike the skin of anyone on the island . . .

Except one person.

Count Monroe.

The count's skin was white—beneath all the freckles and liver spots . . .

The puzzle pieces slipped into place, painting a different picture of the man who'd seemed so kind. That was why he knew so much about singing, why he'd defended the idea of taking energy from a tree. It also explained why he understood how energy could be exchanged. But how was he still alive?

Her stomach heaved as she remembered the way he'd looked at Anatolian playing in the water. The years had fallen off him and she could see it now in her mind's eye. He could be that man the trees had been showing her.

Was it possible the count had used the energy he drained from living things to keep himself alive for two hundred years?

She didn't want to believe it. He'd seemed such a kind old man, holding her hand when she'd been hurt—

"So you've found me out."

Mayten's eyes flew open, terror racing through her like a lightning bolt. She glanced up and recoiled against the tree, rough bark pressing painfully into her back. The count towered over her.

"I can listen to the trees too." He gave her a smile but his eyes stayed cold.

He looks like a cat who's cornered a mouse.

The tall, lean man the tree had shown her was now shrunken and puffy with age. His black curls, what was left of them, had gone gray. But his eyes held that same haughty look.

"You've forgotten your cane." The words sounded silly even to her but she had to say something, somehow get him talking. Her legs had fallen asleep and she needed time to wake them up. Right now, he held the advantage, especially since she couldn't even run.

Mayten slowly unfolded her legs, pain slicing through them as the feeling returned. "You've been draining trees for two hundred years?"

The count clapped slowly, the staccato sound echoing off the trees. "I knew you were a smart girl."

Her legs went from being totally numb to the 'being stabbed with needles' stage.

"Where did you go back then when the king sent you away?" She rolled onto her knees.

"I traveled the world." He looked as though they were discussing his health over tea. "Unfortunately, I wore out my welcome in many different countries." His grin told her he wasn't sorry, wasn't sorry at all.

She startled when he took her hand and helped her to her feet.

"Why did you come back here?" Her voice quavered and her knees almost gave out. How far was she from the lake? Would anyone hear her scream?

"Ah." The count's grin widened.

Like a cat playing with a mouse before he eats it.

"I tired of the taste of orange trees." He laughed.

Bile burned her throat as Mayten realized the citrus she'd always smelled when he was around was *not* cologne.

"You know," he said wistfully, "there is nothing quite like the taste of pine, except the old-growth redwoods, of course."

Her heart hammered against her ribs. She had to get away, had to get help. She kicked, her foot connecting with his shin. He yelped as she turned to run. Before she could take more than a step, his hand grabbed her wrist in a vice-like grip.

Mayten shrieked.

"Are you okay?" Nan ran towards her, notebook in hand. She must have been taking notes nearby. A sprig of pine needles stuck out of her messy hair. How much had she heard?

"She's hurt," the count said.

"Run!" Mayten screamed at the same time. "He's the singer, Nan. The one draining the trees of their life!"

But it was too late. Nan had come too close. The count snatched hold of the princess's wrist and yanked her close.

Mayten struggled to pull away, but could not move. He'd connected to her somehow. Put a hook in her soul and was tugging on that hook, trying to wrench her soul clear out of her body.

Judging by the look on Nan's face, the princess was having the same experience.

How could a two-hundred-year-old man be so strong?

"There's really only one thing better than a pine tree." The count continued. "It wasn't just the prince's dog who died. I took one of the maids as well. The head housekeeper thought she'd just run off. The taste of the human spirit is quite something. It's very . . ." the count paused and drew in a breath as if savoring the smell of a roast pig, "intoxicating. You've had a taste of it yourself, haven't you, Mayten?"

Mayten spat at him in disgust. "I'm not like you!"

Guilt soured her for a long moment. It was true. When she'd healed Rafe, she'd tasted his energy. And had wanted more.

But she hadn't taken it. Not then. Not ever.

"Once you start, you really can't stop," the count continued. "The taste will haunt your dreams. And each person has their own flavor. You, Mayten, are particularly sweet. I must admit I indulged a bit the other night."

The night after she'd been overwhelmed by the memories of the old-growth redwood, Mayten realized. This . . . *man* . . . had held her hand while she slept. No wonder she'd been so drained.

"The princess here tastes more like a fine scotch." The count had the temerity to kiss the back of Nan's hand.

Nan's face grew so pale Mayten was afraid she'd topple over.

"Stop," she demanded, focusing her attention on the count. She could feel him, then. Feel his life energy—

"You are not strong enough . . . or wise enough . . . to beat me!"

Pain dragged at Mayten, as though something tore at her insides. She lost the hold she had on the count's energy as her life force drained away.

CHAPTER THIRTY-ONE

Mayten felt herself weakening against the count's attack. Her knees buckled, her body wanted sleep, her eyes drifted closed.

The sound of pounding feet broke through the haze that seemed to be everywhere. She forced her eyes open and struggled to see what was happening. The prince was running toward them, eyes wide, mouth open.

"Let go of my sister!" The prince's voice, wild and filled with . . . fear?

"What is this?" Adven's growl, fiercer than ever and a bit . . . confused? He ran toward them from another direction, deep lines of concern on his face.

She opened her mouth, tried to shout a warning as the pair raced up, but the words seemed trapped in her throat. She felt more than saw the prince and Adven make the same mistake, grabbing at the count's wrist and arm.

Both went still as frozen statues.

"How nice. A foursome." The count's chuckle pierced Mayten's soul. "I've never had more than two at once. This should be delectable."

Images flickered in and out of her mind. Trees drained of life, animals, people she did not know . . . those who'd given their lives so the count could live?

She could *feel* Adven and the prince resisting, the princess weakening . . .

This was all her fault. Mayten had known something was *off* about the count yesterday when she'd gotten a glimpse of him watching Anatolian at play. He'd looked so young in that moment, so familiar.

But she hadn't made the connection to the face in her vision. Not then. Yes, she'd suspected the singer was close by. She'd even suspected Rafe. She should have told Adven of her suspicions . . .

But the count always seemed so friendly, so kind . . .

Nothing like the man looming over her, anticipation and greed dancing in his eyes. Soon they would all be nothing but empty husks drained of their life energy.

Why oh why hadn't she listened to her gut? Made the others turn around, report back to the king.

Go back home.

You wanted approval, that's why. And now you've failed in your quest, disappointed the king, your clan, and your mother. These folks are going to die because you failed—

:Use your skill, Daughter.:

The voice was so faint it took a moment for Mayten to realize it had even spoken. One of the trees? Her mother?

Thinking of her mother was enough to help her focus. *She* had the ability to draw energy just like the count did.

Could she weaken the man? Somehow get away?

Taking energy is against the Singer's Code, a little voice in her head whispered. *The only offense worthy of death.*

Was she willing to become a murderer to save the others?

Self-defense is not murder. A different voice, stronger this time. Definitely not her mother. One of the trees?

"Stop fighting, little singer," the count hissed. "It'll be much easier if you just let go."

Emotions swirled through her body, interrupting her thoughts, plunging her first into despair (how she missed her family), then into guilt (why had she left her mother without telling her how much she loved her?), stirring up hurt (why did Adven hate her so?), dredging up grief (would she ever stop crying when she thought about Hunter?) and . . . other feelings (like how her stomach fluttered when the prince smiled at her).

Unfamiliar images and emotions pelted her from all sides— betrayal as a man she'd never seen before yet felt that she loved had chosen to join with her sister so she decided to study . . . plants?

Those are Nan's emotions. Nan's memories. Being drained from her along with her life energy. The princess was slipping away.

Mayten focused on the count's hand, feeling each finger where they gripped. She could not—*would* not—let the count win. It didn't matter that taking energy was against her code. Her friends' lives were at stake.

Life energy is your specialty, she reminded herself. No one here knew energy like she did.

Except the count.

She forced herself to relax, to slip into the same focused state she used when conversing with the trees . . .

And immediately felt her energy rushing away. The world spun and she was suddenly oh, so tired. If she could only let go for a moment . . . She couldn't do this alone. She didn't have the training, didn't have the strength . . .

More images pelted her mind and she found herself gazing at her mother, a much younger version who looked very much like the reflection Mayten saw in the mirror every day. She'd never seen her mother this young . . .

These are Adven's memories.

The questor had been in love with her mother.

The images tumbled over each other, leaving brief impressions behind—Mother joining with Da; Adven running off into the woods . . .

He'd run into a bear and had half his face ripped off, almost dying during the healing.

No wonder he hates me. I look just like my mother.

No wonder her mother had chosen not to come on this mission. She and Adven had a history together.

Explains why he hates singers.

More images swirled through her mind, shifting her focus from Adven to . . . the prince? He appeared to be gazing at someone he felt a strong attraction to—

Shock set her skin tingling. The face he fixated on was hers! Not Cather's. Not someone else.

Her.

She got the impression he'd found her beautiful—beautiful!—the first moment he'd seen her—

Nan groaned. Mayten could feel the princess sagging to the ground, energy ebbing so low she could barely sense it.

She had to *do* something, but what? The count was older, wiser, stronger, and she was only a girl . . .

:*You aren't alone, Daughter. We're here, standing beside you.*:

An image of her family in their thanks-giving circle flowed into her mind, their bare feet connected to the earth and sky and everything in between, a place of love, strength, and identity.

I am not *alone.* She had the trees, she had her family and the wisdom of a long line of singers, and she had her friends, her *team.*

:*Help the princess.*: She sent out the cry mentally, reaching for her connection to the trees.

Would it work?

She listened for a reply . . . and felt energy surge through her feet into her body. She could feel the energy flow through to the others. Nan gasped as the pungent smell of pine filled the air.

"What are you doing?" The count glared at her, sweat beading his forehead.

She ignored him.

"We have to fight him together," she gasped. "Combine our strengths and push him back."

Out of the corner of her eye, she saw Adven give a slight nod. The prince didn't move, jaws clenched as though it took all his strength just to keep standing. Nan's eyes were dazed as though she couldn't quite grasp what was happening.

The count snorted. "You can't fight me. You don't know how—"

Mayten took a deep breath, willing herself to have faith. In herself and in her friends. All of them. "Now!"

Energy seemed to form a wall within her, blocking any intrusion. She closed her eyes, picturing a large log needing to be moved. Keeping the log in focus, she imagined herself moving that log, bending to put her hands on it, using her legs for strength as she pushed. She felt her muscles quiver, her arms start to ache . . .

The log moved.

:*Like this.*: Quickly, Mayten expanded her focus, including her four friends in the vision, *willing* them to understand. In her vision they were all pushing logs, pushing with all their strength—

Without warning, the imaginary logs picked up momentum and rolled on their own . . . as if they were rolling downhill!

It was working!

The count's smile vanished. His eyes closed and his lips pressed together in a tight line as if experiencing great pain.

Anatolian barreled into them, barking and snarling. The enormous dog grabbed one of the count's wrists in his jaws.

Snap!

The sound echoed through Mayten's head . . . and the count crumpled to the ground.

Mayten fell to her knees beside him, clutching her chest and struggling to catch her breath. Gasps rose around her as the others did the same. Someone sobbed—Nan?—and Adven let out a curse.

Cautiously, Mayten opened her senses. The sense of being drained had vanished, but she didn't want to open herself up to another attack . . .

:*He's gone.*:

Startled, she glanced around. Which one of the trees had spoken? Which one had helped?

:*All of us. We are you and you are we. There exists no difference between us.*:

"He's dead." Adven's hoarse voice wasn't exactly gleeful. He sounded more . . . satisfied.

The count lay on his back, empty eyes staring up at the sky. No one said a word as his skin began to darken, turning sickly gray, then falling off in chunks.

Nan gasped and buried her head in the prince's shoulder. A moment later, her scientist mind seemed to override her horror and she turned back to watch.

Disgust twisted Mayten's stomach as the count's flesh shrank, pulling back from his cheekbones and skull, then from his entire skeleton. Within seconds, his clothes covered no more than a pile of dust and bones.

Tiny taproots rose from the ground, snaking over bone and cloth until what was left of the count was completely wrapped in roots. With a slight snick! the roots drew him into the soft earth.

In less than three heartbeats, the only evidence left that the count had existed were his hat and boots.

Anatolian snuffled the ground where the count had disappeared, then shot Mayten a disapproving look.

"I didn't do it!" She held her hands out to either side as if showing him she wasn't hiding the count in her hands or sleeves.

"What in God's name just happened?" Adven staggered to his feet.

Mayten shuddered and somehow managed to keep from burying her face in Anatolian's fur. "The cou—"

She cleared her throat. "The count was the evil singer, the one sucking life from the trees. He'd kept himself alive that way for over two hundred years! By taking life from trees, animals, and . . . people."

She shivered now that she knew just how awful an experience it would have been for the poor trees!

"I saw, the—pictures or whatever they were." Adven waved at the ground where the count had been only moments before. "I mean *that!*"

"Accelerated decomposition," Nan said in a flat voice. "When we . . . pushed . . . back, it felt like something snapped, didn't it? Whatever that might have been . . . was enough to kill him. If he's truly two hundred years old, his . . . disintegration was simply nature catching up with him."

The prince stood, helping Nan to her feet.

"Is that what it's like when you talk to trees," the prince asked. "All those pictures . . ."

Mayten used Anatolian's back for support as she stood, legs quivering. She felt as though she'd run for miles. "No, not exactly, thank the stars. Our communication is not usually that intense. It's just a gentle conversation, a two-way flow of energy and images."

"No wonder you didn't want to talk to anyone when you got back the other day. You said that ancient tree shared a lot of memories." The prince shook his head. "I still feel like I'm in shock. What he did!"

He scrubbed his eyes with a hand as if trying to clear away the images.

Adven picked up the boots and hat and headed back to camp. The prince went after him, picking up the cane a few paces from the tree.

Three items. All that was left of the count.

Mayten winced as she followed Adven. Her body felt like it had just survived a physical beating. In fact, they all looked a bit sore.

They walked back to camp, the fire burning to low embers and Rafe sitting near it, his back against a tree.

"What happened?" Rafe asked as they gingerly settled around the fire, Adven adding logs.

Mayten let the others tell the story, jumping in to fill gaps the others didn't know. Rafe asked question after question until they were all talked out. Each seemed lost in their own thoughts, staring in stunned silence at the fire.

Now that the excitement was over, she felt as though the count had succeeded instead of failing. "I'm sorry you all had to go through that."

She stared down at her trembling hands. "I should have figured it out sooner."

"That was terrifying." Nan gave her an apologetic smile. "I had no idea . . ."

"It felt like someone opened a vein and all my blood was draining out," the prince said.

"That's almost exactly what he was doing," Mayten said. "Only instead of blood, he was draining your life energy, something that is against everything we singers believe."

She wanted—no, *needed*—them to understand. The count was a sick man, the exception, not the rule. "A singer's job is to help the life force of living things grow, not to drain it. I never knew such an evil person existed until we came to the castle. Taking life like that—it is the only offense that can lead to death for a singer. Luckily, draining four people at once was more difficult than he expected."

"And he didn't factor in Anatolian." Adven scratched the dog's ears. Anatolian happily thumped his tail.

That was probably the nicest thing Adven had said, even if he'd said it to her dog.

Mayten's eyes teared. "I was fairly sure I knew *what* was happening. I just wasn't sure who was doing it. And I definitely didn't know what to do about it."

"That *count* had us all fooled," Adven said, giving her a nod. "I think we'll stay here tonight. Think you're well enough to rustle up some dinner, Rafe?"

Rafe nodded and the others got to their feet to gather wood. Mayten sat a moment longer, stunned by Adven's comment. Had she finally earned his respect?

CHAPTER THIRTY-TWO

Mayten woke to a strange sensation . . . as if something was calling her to rise and come. Though the sky was still dark, the air filled with predawn chill and the scent of damp earth, she crawled out of her blanket and stumbled to the closest pine tree, trying not to wake the others.

Anatolian huffed in concern. He trotted over to her side and pressed his warm, shaggy body against her.

Appreciating the warmth, she stroked the dog's head, then wrapped her arms around the tree's trunk. Rough bark scratched her hands and wrists and the scent of vanilla filled her nose. All sensation faded when she realized the trees were singing! Rejoicing over the death of the evil one . . .

Over and over, her face reflected in the visions shared by the trees. She didn't understand at first—

She was being honored! As the one who'd defeated the man who'd been killing trees for centuries!

Mayten closed her eyes and let her spirit soar with the song. Sensations thrilled through her—the joy of spring, the birth of a baby, the first steps of a newborn fawn—bringing her spirit into the tree, becoming one with the spirit she touched and each of the spirits beyond—trees, plants, and animals—all the entities of the island . . .

Until she lost her sense of self, becoming a part of all that was.

She didn't know when she had joined the song. She sang light notes that bounced and moved with joy, her voice joining theirs in jubilant melody, filling her with energy and relief, healing and love.

Slowly she became aware of the others behind her. She turned toward the camp. Met the gaze of four pairs of eyes, wide with wonder.

"They're happy." Mayten brushed tears from her face and gestured around her. "The trees are happy."

✍

The trek back to the castle was somber, almost holy. Mayten wrapped Rafe's leg and he used the count's cane as they walked. His leg wasn't giving him too much trouble and they moved steadily along.

Adven carried the count's hat and boots in a blanket tied to his pack. He'd slowed until she caught up. They'd walked quietly side by side for what seemed forever. Adven was quiet as they trudged downhill, seeming lost in his own thoughts. For the first time, his silence felt *easy* instead of angry.

"Should be back in time for dinner." He glanced at her with an unreadable expression.

Why had he decided to walk with her? He'd stayed as far from Mayten as he could ever since leaving their village.

Behind them, Nan and the prince—Mayten had a difficult time calling him 'Tom'—were deep in conversation.

Adven opened his mouth, closed it, opened it again. "So," he stopped, cleared his throat. "You know . . . about your mother and me."

"Yes." She remembered how he'd run into the woods and been hurt by the bear.

They walked in awkward silence. Now she knew why he'd been so hurtful, but what could she do to change that?

"It wasn't just your mother," he finally said. "I've never talked about it, but . . . my mother was a singer."

"What?" Mayten stared at him in amazement.

He nodded, keeping his gaze on the trail. "She left us when I was a boy. Took off with a sailor and left us to fend for ourselves with a da who favored the drink."

Tray's grandparents, Mayten realized. Tray never talked about his grandparents much. Now she knew why.

"No wonder you don't like me," she finally said.

"It's not you," Adven said. "I just told you—it's me. I'm sorry I was such a bear."

The birds chirped high above them while squirrels chattered noisily, chasing each other from tree to tree. Anatolian chased anything that moved.

She bumped him with her elbow. "Hey, you could have been my da!"

He gave her a look of disgust, stepping away in shock.

"Never!" he barked, but Mayten saw the corner of his mouth lift just a bit.

They walked a bit further, then he looked at her, his eyes glimmering. "Thank you for giving Hunter a last Thanks-giving. He was at peace after you left. I . . . gave him some herbs . . . and waited until he, he . . . fell asleep. He didn't wake up."

She took his arm as they walked and gave it a reassuring squeeze. "I'm glad you were with him."

They continued to walk in companionable silence.

"You should forgive your ma, ya know?" he surprised her by saying. "It wasn't her fault you had to come. I told Solis that I wouldn't lead the quest if your ma came. She had no choice but to send you. Said you were the next best singer."

Her mother had no choice?

Now that she knew their history, that statement made sense. She should have realized her mother would have come if she could have, especially if she knew how dangerous their quest would be.

"You should forgive her, too . . . And your own ma." Mayten held her breath. Had she just violated their little truce?

Adven walked in silence, keeping his eyes straight ahead. Finally, he gave a curt nod. "You're right. I think it's time for a lunch break."

CHAPTER THIRTY-THREE

Nan caught up with her after lunch, her step lighter, her body looking more relaxed than when they started this quest. Nan took Adven's place as they walked. "Tom says you might come back in a few years and train some singers."

Mayten laughed. "That's what your da wants, anyway."

"A king usually gets . . ." Nan started in a singsong voice.

". . . what a king wants." Mayten finished. They both laughed.

Nan seemed different today, as though she'd been tucked inside a hard shell and had finally broken free.

"If you do come," Nan continued, "do you think I'm too old to learn how to sing to the plants?"

"No one is too old," Mayten said. "It just takes time."

Nan's eyes sparkled. "Can you imagine combining what I've learned about plants through science and what you know about plants through singing?"

Mayten couldn't resist smiling back. She'd have to talk to her da about this. "I'll make you a deal—I'll come back with some apprentice singers from my clan and start teaching future singers and you can teach us botany!"

Nan looked so excited Mayten wouldn't have been surprised to see the princess break into a jig. "That would be amazing! In fact, I could start teaching one of my sisters or maybe one of the servants' or soldiers' children about botany now, and then they could be apprentices with your family."

Nan wandered up the path, a thoughtful expression on her face.

Probably daydreaming about teaching botany.

Mayten looked up to find the prince walking beside her, an embarrassed grin on his face, and her stomach fluttered as though filled with butterflies.

The prince fiddled with his pack's shoulder straps, adjusting them, then adjusting them again.

"Guess you didn't like me much when we first met." He jerked the straps, scowled, and stopped fiddling.

She grimaced. Looked like the visions she'd received during the whole *count* thing had gone both ways. "No, not really."

He nodded. "I . . . was a bit of a jerk. Bad day and all that."

A squirrel scampered past, leaping on a tree ahead and scrambling up, Anatolian right on its tail. They both laughed.

"I'm going to ask my dad if I can come back with you, you know, to train with Adven as a quester."

"That's nice," she said. Nice? What a lame thing to say. Where was Cather when she needed her? "I mean, that's good. You'll make a good quester."

"I guess I'll get to see you more if I'm there training, you know, in your clan."

"Guess so," she agreed. Why couldn't she come up with something brilliant to say? She sounded like a ninny.

They rounded a corner and she was shocked to see the pond where they'd first met the prince. The afternoon sun made it sparkle like a gem. Mayten felt her face grow hot. She glanced at the prince whose face looked as red as hers felt.

"I'll run ahead to tell them we're home and to prepare dinner for us." The prince took off running without another word.

CHAPTER THIRTY-FOUR

Though the king had been a bit reluctant, the questing team set out again the next day, each of them anxious to get home for their own reasons. There were many hugs from the children and requests to return soon.

The return trip took six days.

Mayten's feet hurt, and she was sick of eating meat again, but it had been a much better trip. The weather had been perfect, Adven wasn't so surly, Cather and Tray were enjoying their time together.

To her surprise, the king had agreed to let the prince apprentice with Adven and had sent two woodsmen with them to cook and hunt.

Though their silences had grown less awkward, Mayten still had a difficult time talking to the prince. She glanced at him out of the corner of her eye, studied the way his dark hair shone as they walked through ribbons of sunlight. The scent of sugar pine whispered of home. Adven was somewhere up ahead. Cather and Tray were behind him. Judging by Tray's waving arms, he was entertaining Cather with another wild adventure.

"There's something I've wanted to ask you," Mayten said without thinking. She glanced at the prince.

"What is it?"

"Where did your siblings get all those silly nicknames and why don't you have one?"

The prince chuckled. "You probably noticed my dad's sense of humor."

She nodded.

"When we got old enough to complain about the Thomas and Thomasina thing, he decided to give us nicknames. And he named us after fruit!"

"Fruit? You mean like Cherry?"

"That's right. He called her Cherry because of her red hair. Nan is Banana."

Mayten laughed so hard she thought her sides would burst. Banana!

"He just kept on going. Lemmy is Lemon, Limey is Lime, Blue is Blueberry and Raz is Raspberry. My baby sister is Plum."

"I guess I should have figured that out," she admitted. "But you didn't say what your nickname is."

"Tom, of course."

He pretended to study a tree close by.

"Do I have to ask Nan? When she hears about Banana—"

"Okay, okay. But you can't tell anyone else. I fought long and hard to be called Tom."

"I promise," she said, raising her hand with a grin.

"It's Ki."

"Ki?"

He rolled his eyes. "Short for Kiwi."

"Kiwi?" She swallowed hard, struggling to keep from laughing.

"Tom," Adven called from somewhere ahead.

"Gotta go," he said, his eyes sparkling. He started to jog away, then turned back. "Remember—you promised." He pointed his finger at her and jogged off.

Cather turned and waited for Mayten, taking her hand when she caught up. "I'm sorry we haven't had much time to talk. The king wanted me to stay with the queen right up until we left. He was really worried about her."

An image of last night's dinner came to mind. A celebration, the king had called it. The queen had been there, too, a babe sleeping in a basket next to her chair. She was beautiful, a reflection of the prince with some laugh lines added, and had seemed to glow with health.

"You worked your magic." Mayten smiled at her friend.

Cather smiled, her dimples showing. "I don't think queens have many people they can talk to. All the castle healers are men, and she didn't want to burden her husband. She mostly needed someone to listen, needed to talk about the children she's lost and how exhausted she is."

"I never thought about how isolated she must be."

"Family and servants, and she doesn't feel comfortable sharing that kind of pain with the servants."

"Is that what healed her? Listening?"

"Her body is worn out from birthing. I gave her the herbs she needs to keep from getting pregnant. I think just having a choice gave her strength and hope. I also think that's one reason she is excited about the school idea. She could have more kids around without having to give birth to them."

Just thinking about the school—suggested by Nan at dinner and approved by the king immediately—made her excited and nervous and a bit overwhelmed. Nan wanted a school for all the callings, not just singing and botany.

Having his queen at the table had put the king in an exceptional mood. He'd toasted their success, his wife's loveliness— and had approved the school as well as . . . Tom's . . . apprenticeship.

A commotion ahead—one of the woodsmen?—made Mayten pause. She put out a hand, holding Cather back. Had something happened . . .

To her relief, Rafe stepped out of the woods. Holding a rabbit. He'd looked confused and more than a bit awkward at dinner last night, but he seemed to be on the mend.

"Do you think I was wrong to try and heal Rafe?" The guilt she'd felt at overstepping her training had kept Mayten awake even after their lovely dinner.

"You didn't try, Mayten." Cather rolled her eyes. "You healed him. I couldn't have done it any better. And no, I don't think it's wrong. Odd that no one has thought of that before. I think it's a wonderful skill to have. And I love that you want to cross-train others. I hope the elders agree."

Mayten was afraid to ask the next question. "When I healed him, when I . . . it's like I tasted his human spirit . . ."

"It tastes good, right?" Cather said the words as if they were common fact.

"Yes. But . . . are you ever tempted to *take* that spirit? Like the count was doing?" Something else that had been keeping her awake at night. She remembered the count's words—

"We take a vow." Cather looked more serious than Mayten had ever seen her. "We vow never to take from our patients, only to give. It's a choice, and not hard once you make that choice."

Fear lifted from Mayten's heart, leaving her feeling giddy. Of course, it was a choice, just like the tree singers made a pledge not to harm the plants.

Anatolian bounded past just as a field of small purple flowers spread before them.

"Listen." Cather held up her hand. A broad smile spread across her face.

Was she hearing the trees? A light melody had followed them on their trek home, fading then growing more intense—

Then she heard it. Not trees. Human voices. Raised in song.

The clan was singing them home!

She grabbed Cather's hand and started to run.

It seemed like forever and no time at all before they broke out of the forest into the square. The entire clan had gathered where the stage used to stand.

"We welcome you back with open arms, our hearts rejoice at your return."

Mayten searched the crowd as the song drew her in. A figure broke from the crowd, running toward her with open arms.

Mother!

Mayten broke into a run, and they collided in a mix of arms and laughter and tears. Mother kissed Mayten's face as if she'd come back from the dead while she touched her mother's face.

"I'm so sorry, Mother."

"Nonsense," her mother said. "It is me who is sorry."

Small arms wrapped around her knees. Mayten pulled back gently from her mother's embrace, smiling down at Wollemi.

"I knew you were okay," he said. A new tooth peeked out where the gap had been. "I asked the stars to watch over you every night."

Mayten kneeled beside her little brother, tears again clouding her eyes. "I can't tell you how much it helped to know you were with me. When I got lonely, I'd look at the stars and know you were there."

He grinned.

A light touch on her arm brought Mayten back to her feet. Taiwania looked at her hesitantly. Mayten pulled her sister into a hug, not knowing what to say. But the trees had taught her how to share, so she opened her heart to her sister.

She didn't hesitate to share her jealousy of Taiwania's beauty and standing in the community. Mayten wanted to start over with her sister. The images she received in return set her back on her heels. Taiwania was jealous of *her*, of her close relationship with her da, and the training that took so much of her mother's time.

Mayten pulled back and the two looked at each other in shock. How much time they had wasted.

"I don't know what just happened," Taiwania said, "but thank you."

Mayten smiled, brushing the hair back from her sister's lovely face. "I've missed you!"

They laughed and hugged again.

"We are so proud of you, Mayten," Mother said. "The trees are singing your praises. And to reach Level Seven, Unity! I want to hear all about it."

Level Seven? Mayten looked at her mother in confusion. Is that what happened when she'd joined with the trees?

The pride in her mother's face drew tears to her eyes once again, but this . . . pride . . . was different. No longer was Mother looking at her as a child, but more as an equal.

The rest of the family crowded around—her still-pregnant sisters, Oleaster with the widest smile she'd ever seen. Da, face streaked with tears, pulled her into a bear hug. Anatolian raced about, barking in excitement and receiving all the petting he was due.

She noticed the prince standing off to one side, looking lost. She waved him over.

"Mind your manners, everyone."

To her surprise, the commotion quieted.

"This is Prince Thomas of Castle Trigginsfeld. He's going to be training with Adven and studying to be a quester."

She watched as her family greeted the prince, some hesitantly, some—namely Wollemi—with enthusiasm.

She was not a child anymore, Mayten realized. She had grown up, learned that there was more to life than simply living on the homestead. She had more friends, now. A better understanding of the world. But one thing was certain.

This village, this clan, would always be *home*.

ACKNOWLEDGEMENTS

Tree Singer is my favorite book to date. I started writing it years ago while sitting at my beloved retreat center, Mercy Center, and staring out at the beautiful trees. I miss being there during this pandemic experience and long to return. Most of my books have been worked on in that peaceful place.

Much thanks to my editor, Louisa Swann, who makes me a better writer and always says, "Where are we now? I need sensory details." How do I always forget those? She was kind enough to come out of retirement for this book. I wonder if she regrets it? She worked hard to get my book and I into shape! I always feel like they are "our" books in the end, though she gets little credit.

Thank you to my early beta readers: Brett Copeland, Jodie Ruana, Patty Doty, Mark Holloman, George Perrault, David Turner and Sarah DeLacey.

Thanks to my more recent beta readers, my SCBWI critique group: Suzanne Morgan Williams and Linda Kay Hardie and those who helped at the end.

A special thank you to my advance team who have been incredibly helpful and encouraging! Kiara Rasmussen, Heather Eaton, Jade Griffin, Jessica Starks, Cheryl Zollinger, Molly Ellen Stewart, Thea Riley, Caryn Lockhart, Marleta, Jack Childress,

Anna Marshall, Alli Miller, Rene Averette, Lesa Larkin, Dante Sellman, Sue C Dugan, Kelli Akers Broberg, Rittie Katz, Cindy Moss Harbolt, Adelai C. Sanborn, Michael Paul, Annette Lambert Lane, Jenetah Walker-Taylor, David Katz, Theresa Borges, Sherry, Miguel Angel Morales, Colleen Koester, Grace Abigail Kengle, and Susie Veon.

As we were editing this book, many of California's forests were on fire. My heart broke over the great losses. But as we see in this book, trees are survivors. I'm thankful we still have the giants among us.

Thank you to my friends at Lucky Bat Books who have championed my writing for eleven years and to my cover designer, Esther Rodriquez aka Merc76 at 99 Designs, who was very patient as we worked to get details to her during the pandemic.

Thanks to God, whom I always feel closest to when I walk among the trees, and to all my fellow tree huggers out there who understand what I mean. May peace and health be yours.

ABOUT THE AUTHOR

Jacci lives in the Nevada desert with her husband and their dog Rosie. She loves to escape as often as possible to the redwood forests in California to walk among the giants and find peace. She also loves chocolate, babies, and writing books for readers of all ages!

For more on Jacci's books go to:
http://jacciturner.com

Look for Jacci on your favorite social media sites:

Facebook:
https://www.facebook.com/pages/Jacci-Turner/162842543809329?fref=ts

Twitter:
https://twitter.com/JacciTurner

YouTube:
https://www.youtube.com/channel/UCU37EJn8r6-o32v-sU697SWg

Pinterest:
https://www.pinterest.com/jacciturner/

Instagram:
https://instagram.com/jacciturner/

http://about.me/jacciturner

Tumblr:
https://www.tumblr.com/blog/jacciturner

Linkedin:
https://www.linkedin.com/profile/view?id=148218545&trk=nav_responsive_tab_profile

Goodreads:
https://www.goodreads.com/author/show/5347211.Jacci_Turner

Made in the USA
Middletown, DE
25 April 2021